BEACHFRONT BAKERY:

A CALAMITOUS COOKIE

(A Beachfront Bakery Cozy Mystery —Book Six)

FIONA GRACE

Fiona Grace

Debut author Fiona Grace is author of the LACEY DOYLE COZY MYSTERY series, comprising nine books; of the TUSCAN VINEYARD COZY MYSTERY series, comprising seven books; of the DUBIOUS WITCH COZY MYSTERY series, comprising three; of the BEACHFRONT BAKERY COZY MYSTERY series, comprising six books; and of the CATS AND DOGS COZY MYSTERY series, comprising six books.

Fiona would love to hear from you, so please visit www.fionagraceauthor.com to receive free ebooks, hear the latest news, and stay in touch.

CHAPTER ONE

Ali stood frozen to the spot, blinking with astonishment as she stared at the silhouette of her father standing in the open doorway of the empty pizzeria. She rubbed her eyes, not sure she could believe what she was seeing. Was this some kind of dream? A hallucination? Or was the man standing before her, framed by the moonlight, really her long lost father?

She took a cautious step closer to the open door. The cool, sea breeze tickled her face. In the distance, noisy seagulls squawked to one another, their chorus blending with the sound of gently breaking waves. Something about the moment made Ali feel like she should whisper.

"Dad?" she said, taking another step forward, her footsteps scuffing on the pizzeria's tiled floor and echoing through the vast, empty space. "Is it really you?"

"It's me," the stranger in the doorway replied. "It's Dad."

For all the times Ali had imagined this moment, now that it was here, words suddenly failed her.

In the silence, Richard shifted awkwardly from foot to foot and jammed his hands deep into the pockets of his raggedy cargo pants. His skin, once pale like her own, was now a reddish-tan color, like that of an aged farmer. Time and his nomadic lifestyle had not treated him well. His face was weather-beaten, the scritchy gray stubble on his chin covering patches of sore-looking skin. He looked like he'd come here straight from the Australian outback, which wasn't too bad of an analogy—his last known residence was an RV park in the Mojave Desert, after all.

"Did you drive?" Ali heard herself blurting, before cringing internally. The question seemed so wholly inadequate considering the circumstances. Her long-lost father had just re-appeared into her life, and she was asking about travel. But the conversation had to start somewhere.

Richard Sweet looked as awkward as Ali felt, and nodded, stiffly. "Yes."

Her eyebrows rose. "In your silver bullet trailer?"

He let out a self-conscious chuckle. "No, no, don't worry, I left the RV at *Desert View*. I drove in a normal car."

At the mention of *Desert View,* the memory of her trip there popped back into Ali's mind's eye. She'd gone to the RV park in the Mojave Desert looking for her father, having tracked him to his last known location, only to learn from a bare-footed, banjo-playing nomad that he'd recently left. She'd asked the man to pass her details on to her father when he returned and had been given the painfully blunt response that when it came to Richard Sweet there was no *when,* only an *if.* Ali had left the RV Park crushed, with next to no faith that she would ever trace her father.

"So you—you got my note after all?" she stammered.

"I did. I came straight here. Hence the late hour." He glanced down at his wrist. "Or early hour, I suppose I should say. I didn't think I'd find you awake..."

"We were having a party. It went on late."

"Oh." He smiled. "Any occasion?"

"My friend's leaving party. He's moving to Italy to get married."

Ali pressed her lips shut. The party she'd earlier been enjoying felt suddenly silly and frivolous. After sixteen years of no communication with her father, was *that* really what she wanted to talk about?

She diverted the conversation back to her failed trip to find him in the Mojave Desert. "I really didn't think you'd get my note. It took a bit of persuasion." An edge crept into her tone as she recalled the way the banjo playing man had seemed far more interested in plucking the strings of his instrument and chatting to the whippet dog at his feet than listening to her plight. In fact, as she went back over it in her mind now, Ali realized the whole trip had been a fiasco, a devastatingly crushing blow, and had left her feeling more unmoored when it came to her missing father than ever. "I wasn't sure Banjo Man would pass on the message."

Richard peered at her with chocolate brown eyes she barely recognized and chuckled. "Banjo Man? He'll like that when I tell him."

Ali bristled at his failure to grasp the gravity of what she was saying. "He said you might not be coming back for months," she implored. "*Years,* even."

"This time it just so happened to be days," Richard said, simply, adding a single-shoulder shrug that irked Ali even further.

She blinked at him, filled with conflicting emotions. He hadn't picked up on the subtext of her statement at all, and a sudden realization hit Ali like a sledgehammer to the chest. The man standing in the spotlight of the moon before her—her father—was by all intents and purposes a stranger now. He had a different energy than she

2

remembered, less confidence, less inner strength. He didn't even look like himself anymore. His ears were bigger. His eyes and mouth had been tugged down by the effects of gravity. Was this the reason Teddy had warned her against searching for him? Had her big brother instinctively known the years would shape him into something unrecognizable, not just in terms of his appearance, but in terms of his very essence? Had she made a terrible mistake pursuing this path?

"I've got to say," Richard's voice said, cutting through her worried ruminations, "it surprised me when I saw you were living in Willow Bay now. I took you here when you were a little girl. We rode the Ferris wheel. Do you remember?"

"I remember," Ali replied.

In fact, it was that happy, nostalgic memory of riding the bright yellow Ferris wheel at the end of the pier with him that had made her decide to move to Willow Bay in the first place. But she didn't feel like sharing that particular detail with him right now.

A loaded silence descended.

Richard glanced around at the empty pizzeria. Emilio and his fiancé Maria had just sold the entire contents to Fat Tony, the town's friendly local mobster, so Ali could take on the lease to the empty store and expand her bakery into it. That was the reason she'd decided to enter the store after the party rather than go home to bed; she wanted to stand here and envision her future. Instead, she'd been interrupted by a sudden intrusion from her past.

"Looks like I just caught you," Richard said. "Are you moving out?"

"Oh. No," Ali replied, realizing there'd been a misunderstanding. "I don't *live* here."

She recalled how the contact details she'd given to Banjo Man had been scrawled under duress. Instead of writing her home address, she'd instead given directions to the row of three stores on the little boardwalk alcove where her small bakery sat sandwiched between the two pizzerias. She hadn't written down the name of her store. Or even that it *was* a store, now she thought of it. Her father, the nomad that he was, must have assumed she was living in the pizzeria. But just because he was accustomed to making the most unusual of places into a home didn't mean she was!

"You don't?" Richard asked, looking confused.

"No. I have an apartment down the road. This is a store I just took on the lease for." It occurred to her then that her father didn't even know she owned a bakery. "I'm expanding my bakery. I lease the premises next door."

Richard's eyebrows rose upward with surprise. "You run a bakery?"

She nodded and wrung her hands hesitantly, feeling suddenly shy. Her father had always encouraged her to follow her dreams and she wondered how he'd react to the news she actually had.

"Do you want to see it?" she asked.

"I'd love to," Richard replied.

For the first time since his sudden appearance, Ali suddenly recognized the father of her memories. He was still there, lurking somewhere deep inside his brown eyes, like a prisoner locked away and unable to break free.

She felt something shift in her mind, like frost thawing, and gestured him out of the pizzeria with a little buzz of excitement. She locked the door firmly behind her and guided her father the short distance across the boardwalk to the bakery next door, stealing furtive glances at him as they went.

"It's a bit of a mess at the moment," she said, as she fumbled nervously, trying to get her key in the lock. "Because of the party. There's plenty of leftover cake, if you're hungry."

"And this is a cake you made with your own fair hands?" Richard asked.

"That's right," Ali said.

"Then I'd love some."

Ali smiled, feeling a childish giddiness overcome her. It was a peculiar feeling, one that had lain dormant for a long time. She couldn't even remember the last time she'd wanted to make her father proud of her...

She shoved her shoulder into the door to get it open, then staggered when it finally yielded. "It gets a little stiff," she explained.

Richard followed her inside. His worn leather boots looked out of place on the bakery's quaint peppermint and white checkerboard tiles. Sequin confetti left over from the party sparkled all over the floor. A shimmery foil banner hanging against the wall proclaimed: *Emilio & Maria...That's Amore.* Ali yanked it down, feeling suddenly self-conscious.

Richard stepped further inside and glanced around at the decor. Ali had chosen a shabby chic interior for her bakery, favoring pastel-painted wooden shelves and floral cushions over anything sleek or modern. The checkered curtains hanging in the windows blocked out most of the moonlight, and Ali was quietly glad her father wasn't able to assess her bakery fully. She didn't want him to cast judgement upon the place.

"Have you been here long?" Richard asked. He spoke in an overly formal manner, like he was a property realtor rather than a family member. Ali felt her earlier giddiness start to falter as she realized just how uncomfortable her father felt to be standing in her domain, and the thought caused a flood of grief to wash through her.

"A few months," she told him. "I was able to open the business thanks to a loan from Teddy."

She snapped her lips shut, realizing too late that in mentioning her brother's name she'd pressed on the sorest, rawest spot she possibly could have. Richard and Teddy's last face-to-face meeting had descended into a screaming match of epic proportions. Ali often wondered, had it not been for the argument, perhaps Richard would not have drifted away from them so fully.

"Anyway," she said quickly, eager to get away from any serious topic. "I promised you some cake. I'll be right back. Take a seat." She gestured to the window seat, the favored spot of her best friend, Delaney, and the town stray, Scruff.

As Richard lowered himself onto the wooden box seat, Ali raced away and pushed open the swinging steel doors of the kitchen.

In the cool darkness of the kitchen, Ali's heart was thumping with nervous energy. Having her dad here was really throwing her for a loop.

"Get it together, Ali," she told herself.

She paced across the tiled floor and pulled open the doors to the big industrial fridge. Light blasted from it, along with a chill that made goosebumps sprout along the lengths of her arms.

She retrieved the multi-tiered celebration cake from the fridge and kicked the door closed behind her, then carried the heavy cake over to the metal preparation counter and set it down gently. Her hands shook as she removed the saran wrap and prepared a plate and slice of cake for her father. Was it his anticipated judgement that was making her nervous? Or was it something else — the thought of him disappearing back into the ether as suddenly as he'd appeared from it?

She took a deep breath to settle her nerves, then pushed backwards through the double swing doors into the bakery. She turned, blinking in the unexpected brightness of the store lights.

"You found the lights," she commented.

"Yes. And company."

As Ali's eyes adjusted to the change in brightness, she realized that sitting next to her father at the window seat was none other than Scruff, the boardwalk stray. He lifted his face and barked happily at the sight of Ali.

"Oh!" Ali exclaimed. "That's Scruff. Our friendly local stray." She brought the plate over and slid it onto the table in front of her dad. "Scruff, this is my dad."

He barked again, and Ali took the seat beside him, glad there was now a buffer between her and her father. Trust Scruff to intuitively know that she needed him.

"Well, well, well," Richard said, glancing down at the plate of cake in front of him. "This looks very professional."

"Good to know," Ali said, smiling proudly. "I learned the recipe from a real pastry chef while I was studying in France."

Richard paused, fork hovering over the cake, and his eyes went round with evident astonishment. "You studied in France?"

Ali frowned. "Yes. Why do you say it like it's such a surprise to you?" Did he not think she was clever enough for such an endeavor? Hannah was always the smartest of the Sweet siblings, and Ali had often felt overshadowed by her high-flying older sister.

Richard scratched his chin, clearly uncomfortable with the question. "Well, it's just that…to be honest, it sounds like something your mom would want you to do."

Ali tensed. He was right, of course. It had been at her mother Georgia's insistence that she went abroad to train, just as it had been at her mother's insistence that she get the job at *Eclair's* that she'd grown to loathe. But that was not a topic she wanted to discuss with her father. It didn't feel right. Her mother, for all her faults, had stuck around when he had not. Even though she'd pushed Ali along some of the wrong paths, at least she'd actually been there and cared enough about her life to try. What had Richard done? He'd left when the going got tough!

Ali felt a sudden wave of negativity come over her. Her father had been back in her life for a short amount of time, and already she felt like she'd been spinning round and round on a Ferris wheel with him. She was getting dizzy from the emotional highs and lows.

She grabbed the second fork and helped herself to a huge bite of cake for comfort. It tasted even better than it had a few hours earlier at the party, because the time it had spent in the fridge had made the frosting cool, the sponge firm, and the layer of strawberry jelly even fresher. Plus, if her mouth was full, she wouldn't be able to speak…

As if picking up on the tension, Richard put the fork down carefully. A frown appeared between his eyebrows. He looked at her earnestly. "Ali, I want you to know I'm really sorry about everything. I know I owe you an explanation."

Ali put her own fork down, mirroring him, and wiped the crumbs from the corner of her lips. "You're right. I do have a lot of questions. But I don't know if I want to jump right into it now. It's been a long day and, well, you kind of appeared out of the blue."

From his seat beside her, Scruff barked as if agreeing with it having been a long day. He was clearly picking up on the uncomfortable vibes and knew she needed some moral support. She petted him gratefully.

"It doesn't have to be now," Richard amended, hurriedly. "I've booked a room in town. The Willow Bay Inn. I'll be around for the next few days."

"Days?" Ali echoed, a lump forming in her throat. She tried to swallow it down. One conversation with her father had been hard enough. She didn't know how she'd be able to cope with *days* of this.

Pain registered in Richard's eyes. "I thought maybe we could hang out a bit? Talk? Whenever you're ready."

Ali nodded, slowly. The next few days with her dad in town could potentially turn out to be really stressful. "I'd...I'd like that," she said with uncertainty. "Perhaps we could meet up tomorrow?"

"You mean later today?" Richard replied with a smirk.

"Right, of course," Ali corrected herself. "I keep losing track of time. Everything feels unreal."

Richard drew in a sharp breath, as if her admission had pained him. He rubbed his forehead. "Ali, perhaps if you could just let me explain a few things now..."

Ali's heart started to race. She shook her head, suddenly terrified by the admission that was about to stumble from her father's open mouth.

"Your mother and I...," he began.

But before he could finish the statement, a sudden loud noise came from somewhere outside, startling both him and Ali. Richard turned in his seat, looking toward the source of the awful noise, and in his hurried movements accidentally stuck his elbow in the cake. The china plate went careening off the table to the floor and smashed. Ali jumped a mile, all the sudden abrupt noises making her already heightened sense of anxiety a thousand times worse.

"What is that?" she gasped, jumping out of her seat and darting for the door.

Scruff leaped down from the table and raced behind her to the door, a low growl in his throat. His ears were back, his fur standing on end. Whatever the noise was, it was giving them both the hee-bee-gee-bees.

Ali stuck her head out the door, looking out toward the ocean. The noise was coming from the direction of the beach, and now Ali could distinguish what it was. Screaming.

A feeling of ice swept over Ali. Immediately fearing the worst, she rushed out of her store and headed for the beach. She didn't stop to see whether Scruff or her father had followed, too; she just raced down to the sand. The screams grew louder and louder with every step she took.

"Hello?" she cried into the darkness, her voice trembling. "Do you need help?"

Suddenly, she spotted someone. A man, jumping up and down waving his arms. She ran to him.

"Are you okay? Do you need help?"

The man swirled to face her, his hollering stopping instantly. To Ali's surprise, he was grinning widely from ear to ear. So... definitely *not* dying, then.

Just then, Ali noticed a strange, long object lying in the sand. A metal detector? And then the moonlight bounced off something shiny in the man's palm. It looked like a coin.

Ali put two and two together. The screaming was the sound of celebration. The man was a metal detectorist and he'd just found buried treasure.

All the adrenaline rushed out of Ali's body. Suddenly, she felt exhausted. Maria and Emilio's party had gone on much later than intended, then her dad had shown up out of the blue, and now this. Her nerves were shot.

She turned, seeing her father and Scruff approaching. But where the dog marched confidently toward her, Richard stopped at the edge of the stand, as if holding back.

"I'm going to head to the inn," he called across the distance between them. "But I'll come by the bakery later today, once we're both a bit more rested. We can have that talk."

"Okay, sleep well," Ali called back.

But her father had already turned his back to her and was walking away.

Scruff raced up beside her.

"Come on, boy," she said, taking her store keys out of her pocket. "Let's lock up and go home."

She cast a final glance at the man on the beach who'd alarmed her so thoroughly, then turned back in the direction of the bakery. Her father, she discovered, had already gone.

CHAPTER TWO

Ali's alarm blared her awake later that morning, after just a few measly hours of unrefreshing sleep. She reached out and thwacked the alarm clock on the bedside table into silence, then forced her tired eyes open and blinked up at the ceiling.

Outside her bedroom window, the sound of the swallows' morning song blended with the gentle waves crashing against the shore. But despite the calm tranquility of the beachside California morning, a sudden feeling of nervous dread descended over her.

She sat up in bed, puzzled by the way her heart was pounding and the cold sweat beading the back of her neck. She'd not had a nightmare, so why was she so panicked?

She forced her mind to Emilio and Maria's party the night before, searching for something that might have caused her sudden sense of alarm, perhaps something stupid she'd done while tipsy? But there had been no dancing on the tables from what she recalled. No embarrassing karaoke moments (aside from her and Delaney's duet of Madonna's *Like A Virgin*) ...

Then suddenly, the memory hit Ali and she remembered. It wasn't anything that had happened at the party that was causing her strange sudden panic, it was what happened *after*. Her father's sudden appearance. The screams of the man on the beach that had stopped him just as he was about to reveal the truth of his abandonment. And their poorly organized plan to meet at the bakery at some unspecified time of the day for that long-awaited talk. *That* was why she had woken in a cold sweat.

Ali pulled back the cover, her movement waking Scruff from his slumber at her feet. He tipped his head to the side quizzically and let out a small, concerned *gruff-gruff.*

"I'm fine," Ali assured him. "I just have a lot on my mind..."

She heaved her body out of bed. She'd expected to be tired today because of the party — Emilio and Maria were the partying type, after all, and being the host for such a special occasion was inherently tiring — but she hadn't expected to feel quite so *drained*. All the emotions her father's sudden appearance had dredged up were absolutely exhausting and they'd not even had their talk yet. It felt as if a cloud of emotion had formed above her head and was threatening to rain on her any second.

She went for her morning shower, her thoughts fixed on their planned meeting later that day. After all this time, she should be thrilled about the prospect of spending time with him today, shouldn't she? Of sitting down with him and getting answers to all the questions that had raced around her head for the last sixteen years? But instead, she was nervous. Apprehensive. Conflicted. She didn't understand what exactly she was so worried about, but even the warm sudsy water couldn't wash away the feeling.

As she dried her hair in the mirror, Ali found herself automatically re-assessing her own reflection. Now that she'd finally set eyes on her father's actual face, the blanks in her own aging appearance seemed filled in. She could see how the frown line between her eyes matched his, how the laugh creases beside her mouth were the mirror image of his own. Before, those things had just been by-the-by, no big deal, but now suddenly they took on a significance she couldn't quite fathom.

She worked her wet hair into a thick braid and slung it over her shoulder, then dressed in her pink *Seaside Sweets* T-shirt. As she reached for her favorite comfortable jeans, the thought briefly crossed her mind that she should dress up a little for the meeting with her dad. But then she remembered how he'd looked so disheveled in his baggy cargo pants and leather boots and decided against it. His lack of fashion sense seemed parallel to her own, and she wondered whether it ran in the genes. And to think she'd been so worried about what he might think of her, in her scuffed sneakers and simple jeans.

She left her bedroom and padded on bare feet across the small, carpeted corridor toward the kitchenette. At this time of day, the small, simple kitchen-area overlooking the living room was gloomy, and the basic decor didn't help matters. She'd done her best to make the apartment homey since moving in, with photos of her family and friends pinned to the fridge with magnets and a glass vase of lemons injecting some much-needed color into the apartment, but it was still rather drab. Perhaps once she'd finished with the bakery expansion, she should turn her attention to her apartment?

As she entered the kitchen, she found Scruff waiting expectantly by the cupboard that contained his kibble. His pink tongue lolled, and he wagged his tail excitedly.

Ali chuckled and fetched two cereal bowls down. She filled one with kibble for Scruff, and the other with cereal for herself.

"You do know my apartment isn't actually a B&B, right?" she said, setting the bowl down on the tiles beside his paws.

He barked his thanks and buried his head into the bowl, eagerly and noisily scarfing up his breakfast.

Ali wondered at what point things had switched from him being an occasional visitor to her home to him using it as his preferred spot. He had practically moved in now, and though she'd happily adopt him properly, she knew Scruff was too much of a free spirit to be tied down to only one human.

She filled the cereal bowl with cool milk, then leaned against the counter and ate her breakfast in ponderous silence, getting lost in her thoughts about what her day would hold. The talk with her father. The expansion plans. She already felt like there was more on her plate than she was able to handle, and it took a concerted effort not to let herself become completely overwhelmed by it all.

Just then, the sound of Scruffy's bark pulled her from her worried ruminations. She looked down to find him staring up at her with his big brown eyes. The bowl at his feet had been licked clean.

"Wow, you scarfed that down!" Ali said. But a quick glance at the wall clock told her that actually she had been slow. She must've gotten lost in her thoughts. Quickly, she gulped down the last few mouthfuls of her own breakfast. "Ok. Let's get going."

With a final internal cheer for herself of, *"you can do this,"* Ali ushered the dog toward the front door and grabbed her store keys off the coffee table. They were heavier now thanks to the additional key to the new premises and Ali felt a thrill race through her body about the prospect of turning the space into her own. She'd had a million ideas before, but there was a bit too much percolating around in her head at the moment with her dad's arrival to really jump into the renovations with both feet. Hopefully, her brain would catch up to the fact her dad was a solid human being rather than a ghost that only existed in her memories, and then she'd be able to work on the new premises with the same level of enthusiasm she'd previously had. First, she had to have that long awaited talk with her dad and break the news to Teddy that their dad was back on the scene. And Hannah, come to think of it, though the eldest of the Sweet siblings balked at expressing emotion and would simply act like it was no big deal. Then another thought hit Ali. She would also have to tell her *mom!*

Ali pushed that particularly troublesome task to the bottom of her mental to do list and slid on her sneakers. Then she pulled open the front door and headed outside with Scruff in tow.

As she locked the door to her small seaside apartment behind her, the salty ocean smell wafted into her nostrils, and she decided to take the slightly longer route along the beach to work. It was her preference when she had lots on her mind, and with her father suddenly reappearing in her life, she had even more than usual. Something about the gentle lapping waves and the chattering gulls in the sky always helped calm her troubled mind.

But when she reached the beach, Ali quickly discovered the little piece of tranquility she was craving had been snatched from her. The beach was packed! And not with the usual tourists and locals, but with hordes of people holding metal detectors, walking slowly back and forth waving their machines in front of them.

Ali thought back to the man who'd found the coin in the small hours of the morning. Was this something to do with his discovery? Maybe the coin was a special antique? And with so many treasure hunters on the beach, perhaps that meant there was more gold to be discovered? Was Willow Bay about to have its own gold rush?

Ali watched the treasure hunters with intrigue. They were an eclectic bunch to say the least, a peculiar mix of hippies and beach bums, taking slow, considered steps around the beach with their metal detectors buzzing as they went.

"Would you take a look at that, Scruffy…," she murmured, her naturally curious character rearing its head. "We're hosting treasure hunters!"

But when she looked down for him, she discovered the little dog had disappeared.

She didn't think much of it at first. Scruff had a tendency to dart around the town, from the pier to the boardwalk and beach, searching for kind tourists to donate scraps of food to him. And with so many new, strange faces on the beach, there were plenty of people around for him to flash his big brown begging eyes to. So Ali turned away from the peculiar crowd of treasure hunters and began to head toward the bakery, her mind switching to her tasks of the day — the batches of macarons, cookies, cupcakes, and croissants she needed to make this morning on her own since Piper had taken the morning off.

But she'd not made it very far up the beach when she spotted Scruff. Rather than begging for food and affection like he normally did, he was enthusiastically digging in the sand, kicking clumps of wet sand behind him with his paws, making a hole that grew rapidly deeper. Ali realized he was joining in with the treasure hunter beside him, a young man in a slogan T-shirt proclaiming, *"The truth is out there."* But it didn't look like his efforts to help were appreciated. The man was frustratedly attempting to shoo him away.

With a chuckle at the comical scene, Ali jogged over.

"I'm so sorry," she said to the man with a good-humored tone, taking Scruff by the collar and guiding him out of the hole he'd burrowed. "I think watching you has made him realize it's possible to dig in the sand!"

Scruff snorted, his nose covered in grains of sand, and strained against his collar to get back to his newfound hobby of hole digging.

The man glowered at her. "Is that your dog?" he said gruffly.

"Well, he's kind of the town's dog," she explained. "All of us vendors on the boardwalk take care of him."

The man's eyes grew darker as he narrowed them and put his hands on his hips. "I didn't ask for your life story. I need you to get him away from me. He's a nuisance. And he's a straggly mess. Why don't you give him a bath? There must be a dog groomer somewhere in this ugly little town?"

Ali's eyebrows rose all the way to her hairline with astonishment. She felt offended by this rude, insulting man, for herself, her town, and Scruffy! If this man was anything like the rest of the treasure hunters, she only hoped none of them decided to visit the bakery later, or else she'd be in for a terrible day.

Ali balled her hands into fists. "Come on Scruffy, let's go," she said through gritted teeth. She wanted nothing more to do with the treasure hunting crowd and turned to leave.

But Scruff stayed where he was. He glanced from her to his hole in the sand and wagged his tail eagerly. Now that his little doggy mind had been opened to the idea of *digging* in the *sand*, he'd gotten a taste for it and wanted to stay. But the conspiracy theory man was still standing there glowering at her angrily, looking disgusted by Scruff. They weren't welcome here.

Ali looked down at the dog and tried reasoning with him. "Look, Lil' Dude. I'm sorry but not everyone in the world appreciates a good canine when they meet one." She flashed a pointed glare at the conspiracy theory man who scoffed in response.

Scruff tipped his head to the side quizzically and whined.

"I know," Ali continued. "And I'm sorry. But that's just how it is. You're going to have to quit digging your hole. For now, at least."

Scruff cast a mournful glance toward his beloved hole. The angry treasure hunter huffed and sighed with irritation, and muttered under his breath to no one, "Is this lady crazy? Talking to a dog?" As far as

Ali was concerned, it was much less strange talking to a dog than talking to oneself, but she held her tongue and focused on Scruff and his predicament.

"Hey, I have an idea!" she said as she suddenly thought of the large grassy area out the back of the former pizzeria that now belonged to her. "The garden! You can dig as many holes in the mud as you want!"

Scruff looked unconvinced.

"Mud and sand are pretty similar," Ali assured him. "You'll like it just as much. I promise."

Scruff looked from her to his hole. Then, with a final nostril-flare and huff, he turned from his beloved hole and walked up beside Ali's heels. The treasure hunter sneered with disdain, then went back to his metal detector.

Ali petted Scruff between the ears. "Thanks, boy. You made a big sacrifice giving up your hole but trust me when I say it's better not to hang around people with such negative energy, even when you're a dog."

She cast a final glance at the strange crowd of detectorists, crossing her fingers that the bizarre people would leave the beach sooner rather than later, and headed off the beach with Scruff in the direction of *Seaside Sweets*.

Once they reached the small palm-tree lined alcove off the boardwalk where the bakery and the pizzerias were located, Scruff went straight up to *Emilio's* storefront and began to bark, reminding her of her promise she'd made to let him dig up the garden. She took her keychain from her pocket, and found the new, unfamiliar key among the batch. She opened the door to the pizzeria, and Scruff scurried off into the darkness, his claws making a scritching noise on the tiles as he beelined for the patio doors that led to the garden.

But Ali halted. The second she'd stepped inside the pizzeria, she'd been hit with the memory of that morning, of the moment her father had appeared in the doorway and back into her life, changing everything in the process. It was like the whole world had tilted on its axis, and all the emotions of that moment washed back at her in one sudden wave.

Scruff barked and began to paw at the glass of the French doors. Ali snapped out of her ruminations and hurried to the door, letting Scruff out into the garden. When it was the pizzeria, the space had been utilized as a second dining area with waterproof canopies and heaters, but everything had been sold off to Fat Tony at Ali's request so she could have a blank slate to work with. Had she been in a better frame of mind, she'd be able to picture how she wanted the garden to look — a greenhouse tearoom, rose bushes and buddleias — but thanks to her emotions, her mind was a blank slate. Which was perfect for Scruff, really, because she had no qualms about how many, or how big, the holes he'd enthusiastically begun to dig ended up being.

"Just bark if you need anything," she told him. "I'm just the other side of the fence."

Scruff didn't reply. He was already burrowing into the soil like a rabbit making a warren. Ali decided not to disturb him, since he was happy and occupied, so she went back inside, closed the patio door behind her, and hurried back out of the empty pizzeria, only remembering at the last second that she needed to lock the door.

She had to admit, it was a relief to get inside the bakery. *Seaside Sweets* was like a sanctuary for Ali. Even with all the mess from the party still to tidy up — confetti and streamers — the familiar smell of sugar and dough enveloped her like the warmest, most comfortable hug. She could always count on her precious bakery to make her feel better. No matter what life threw at her, as long as she had the bakery to retreat to, she could weather any storm.

Ali grabbed the brush to sweep up the detritus on the floor. But as soon as she began, her gaze fell to the smashed plate and the smooshed cake, and her mind's eye replayed the moment her father had accidentally swiped it to the ground. Once again, all her worries about their planned talk later that day returned in one sudden rush.

She crouched down and began picking up the broken pieces of china, wondering as she worked what the meeting with her father later that day would hold. If the mere thought of having the talk with him caused her such trepidation, how would she feel once he finally revealed the secret of his sixteen-year disappearance?

CHAPTER THREE

Ali slid the final batch of that morning's pastries into the display cabinet. The bakery was now sparkling clean. The freshly baked cupcakes, rainbow-colored macarons, and range of cookies *Seaside Sweets* had become famous for looked temptingly delicious in the glass display cabinet. The coffee machine hissed and glugged in the background, filling the bakery with the gorgeous aroma of freshly ground beans. Scruff slept in his favorite window seat, evidently exhausted from the last few hours he'd spent digging holes in the garden while getting his paws incredibly muddy. Everything was tranquil, and had this been any normal day, Ali would be feeling eager to open the doors to the customers and get on with another busy day. But instead, the hands of the ticking wall clock inching ever closer to her nine AM opening time filled her with dread, because time was also ticking ever closer to the planned meeting with her father.

Just then, the door opened, making the bell above tinkle. Ali's breath caught in her lungs as she peered up with anticipation, fully expecting to see Richard enter. Instead, it was Piper, her assistant. She came rushing inside, looking fresh and well rested, her silky blond hair shimmering in the early morning sunshine.

"Good morning, Ali!" she exclaimed as she breezed across the peppermint green and white checkerboard tiles on her pale pink ballet pumps. "Thanks so much for giving me the morning off. I got my teeth whitened." She grinned her huge pearly smile, almost dazzling Ali in the process.

"I can see," Ali replied.

Piper passed behind her and collected an apron from the hooks, looping it over her head and tying it in place. "Did you hear the news?" she asked.

Ali frowned. Her assistant seemed almost giddy and wide-eyed as a child on Christmas. "What news?"

"Someone found treasure on the beach!" Piper trilled. "Gold! There's tons of people on the beach now searching for more."

Ali was slightly perplexed by the level of interest Piper was paying to the gold coin. She'd seen this side of Piper before, the ditzy, dazed, glazed-eyed look that overcame her whenever a Z-list celebrity was in town. But she couldn't understand why she was going giddy over a bunch of nerdy metal detectorists.

"Yes, I heard," Ali said, grabbing a cloth and wiping crumbs from the countertop. "Matter of fact, I was there when the coin was found."

"Really?" Piper cried, like this was something marvelous. "What happened?"

Ali hesitated. To tell the story accurately, she'd need to explain *who* she had been with last night when the coin had been discovered. And while Piper had supported her through her whole quest to find her father, the thought of actually telling her he was in town was putting her on edge.

"Actually, it's a funny story…," Ali began, only to be cut off by Piper abruptly shoving a cell phone under her nose.

"It's true!" Piper squealed, nudging the phone so close Ali went cross-eyed.

With a frustrated frown, Ali took it from her and moved it a more comfortable distance from her face, before scanning through the text on the web page displayed on the screen. She read aloud, "*'Antique's Hunters* are confirmed to be filming in California today. Rumors say they will either be in Willow Bay, Haven Bay, or Wave Bay. Check back later for updates!'" She peeped over the cell phone at Piper, bemused. "What's *Antique's Hunters?*"

Piper gasped. "Oh Ali, don't tell me you've never heard of it? It's new and it's going totally viral!"

"Sounds painful," Ali quipped.

Piper let out an exasperated sigh, the one she saved for Ali's "grandma" moments. At twenty-one years old, Piper couldn't understand how anyone so technologically illiterate managed to function in society, especially someone Ali's age. She was only thirty-four, but her aversion to all things social media made her seem closer to eighty-four sometimes.

"Have you been living under a rock?" Piper said. "*Antiques Hunters! Antiques Hunters!*"

"Shouting the name loudly at me won't make me more likely to know it," Ali replied.

Piper scoffed at her cluelessness. "It's hosted by that guy with the '80s haircut!" She mimed what Ali guessed was a mullet with her hands. "You have to know him! He's everywhere."

"And by everywhere, you mean everywhere online? Which is technically nowhere, because the internet isn't actually a *place.*"

Piper rolled her eyes. "Oh Ali, please stop with the philosophy. Don't you see what this means?"

Ali peered ponderously out of the window at the people on the beach. "I guess it means there might be more treasure to discover." She grimaced. "And we'll be forced to endure those treasure hunters for a while longer."

"No, dummy!" Piper cried. "It means I might get the chance to be on TV!"

Ali looked back at Piper. So *that* was why she'd been so starry eyed when she arrived? Piper was an aspiring actress, always searching for her big break moment. She took every opportunity, no matter how small, very seriously. For all her faults — her occasional tactlessness, not to mention her clumsiness in the kitchen — Piper was never deterred when it came to her acting aspirations and Ali had to admire her for it.

But then a sudden thought hit Ali, and she braced herself in anticipation. "You're going to ask for time off, aren't you?"

Piper looked at her hopefully. "Can I? Just while the film crew are around? If I get into enough of the background shots, a talent scout might notice my beauty!" She batted her eyelashes.

Ali sighed. There was so much to do at the moment. She'd hoped Piper would be able to take the reins from her a bit so she could focus on the expansion plans and her father's visit. Her being otherwise engaged would really make a stressful time worse for Ali.

"Please!" Piper suddenly cried, as if reading the hesitation in Ali's eyes. "I'll make it up to you!"

Ali narrowed her eyes. "How?"

Piper's gaze darted around as if searching for inspiration. "Ooh! I know! How about once the crew have left, I do double-lunch shifts? You could take two-hour lunches while I cover the register?"

Ali was about to immediately rebuke the offer since she rarely took the hour she was meant to anyway, but then had a sudden thought. If Piper covered the register for two hours instead of one, she'd be able to use the extra time to work on the old pizzeria, painting and decorating, and really taking her time to get to know the space and make it her own.

Ali looked again into her assistant's hopeful green eyes and relented. How could she say no to her ambitious young friend? She simply couldn't be the one to break her spirit.

"Okay, okay," Ali said. "You can have time off while the film crew are around in exchange for longer lunch cover once they've left."

Piper punched the air. "Thanks, boss!"

"But I have one more condition," Ali added.

"Anything!" Piper exclaimed, putting her hands into a prayer position.

"The show will be filming on the beach, right? In which case, I'd like you to check into the bakery once an hour to see if I need any help. If there's a line out the door or I've sold out of cookies or whatever, I want you to prioritize the bakery. Okay?"

Piper hesitated. "I *can* do that. But I don't want to leave if they do start filming me." She held her hand out to Ali's. "So long as you're okay with that, then it's a deal."

It was far from ideal, but Ali shook on it. "Fine. Deal."

Piper squealed again and jumped up and down on the spot like a hovering hummingbird. "Thank you, Ali! I'm so excited. This could be my big break."

Ali couldn't fathom how lingering around in the background shots of a TV show about antiques of all things might constitute a big break. "Are you really sure about this TV show? Antiques seem very…," she paused, struggling to find the word, before landing on, "unsexy."

"Well, it's not like your normal antiques show," Piper told her. "Just wait 'til they start filming. Then you'll see what I mean."

"And you're *sure* they're even coming to Willow Bay? It says on the website they might be in Haven Bay or Wave Bay."

Piper rolled her eyes. "Did you *see* all the treasure hunters on the beach? Trust me. They're coming." She went back to her cell phone, and started thumbing through it rapidly, cooing with excitement as she went.

Ali shook her head and went back to wiping the counter. Piper being in cuckoo land was far from ideal considering everything else going on at the moment, but at least she'd get something out of it too, with extra time at lunch. Perhaps she could even use the long lunch to have that talk with her dad? He did say he'd be around for a few days, so maybe if she postponed it until after the film crew had left, they could use the two hours to go for a proper sit-down meal at a nice restaurant, and hash out all their feelings over a three-course meal and copious amounts of dessert. Or maybe she was just looking for ways to stall the inevitable?

Ali paused and looked back over at Piper. It was about time she told her what was going on. Piper had been her friend, her confidant, and her support system during all the months she'd been searching for her father, through the highs and lows of new leads and dead ends. She deserved to know that the man at the center of it all was in town and may appear at any second.

But just as Ali prepared herself to break the news about her father, the door opened so abruptly the brass bell above jangled angrily. She started and looked over to see her friend Delaney come rushing in.

"Guess what I have!" the bronzed beauty cried, waving a large scroll of paper over her head, making the myriad of metal bangles on her arms tinkle.

Ali frowned with curiosity at the scroll. "What?"

Delaney flashed her a pearly-toothed grin and rushed forward on her gladiator sandals, her silk paisley patterned skirt swishing around her tanned calves. "Expansion plans!" she exclaimed, dumping the scroll on the counter. "For the pizzeria."

"Plans for the pizzeria?" she echoed with confusion.

Had she tipsily commissioned Delaney to draw up the expansion plans, perhaps after their Madonna duet when her memories became foggy? But then she realized her friend had simply done this out of the goodness of her heart. After all, Delaney had offered her keen eye for interior design to the bakery for free, just to be kind. She'd created all the bakery's cute cartoon characters like Mr. Macaron for fun. Delaney was a creative soul. She thrived any time she flexed her artistic muscles and had evidently thrown herself at the opportunity to reorganize and decorate an empty store as soon as it had presented itself.

"When did you get the time to draw them?" Ali asked. The party had continued until the small hours of the morning. Emilio and Maria's plane probably hadn't even left the runway yet. For Delaney to have created a whole plan in that time was simply miraculous.

But her friend flashed her a devilish look, and said, "I started working on it as soon as Emilio said the lease was available."

Ali frowned with confusion. She hadn't decided to take on the lease for several days after Emilio's announcement, so why had Delaney drawn up a plan that might never have seen the light of day? "But I didn't even know I was going to take on the lease. Wouldn't you have been disappointed if you'd gone to so much trouble when, in the end, I decided against taking on the lease?"

"No…," Delaney said, flashing her a knowing look, "...because *I* always knew you would."

It all started to make sense in Ali's mind. Delaney had so much faith in her, she'd had no doubts.

She smiled shyly at her friend. "You did, did you?"

"Of course!" Delaney exclaimed. "I always knew you'd make the bakery a success and need to expand sooner or later. When Emilio announced he was leaving, I just knew you'd go for it. Eventually. After some gentle coaxing."

Ali grinned at her friend. Sometimes she wondered what she had done to deserve such a kind, supportive friend like Delaney. None of her friends back in LA were ever as sweet or considerate. Having a cheerleader like Delaney on her side really made the troubles in life easier to handle.

"Thank you, Delaney," she said with gratitude, before looking eagerly at the scroll. "So? Can I see?"

"You bet!"

Delaney carefully unfurled the scroll from the middle out with both arms, stretching it wide across the countertop. She weighed down each side with coffee mugs as paper weights to stop it curling back up, then Ali and Piper leaned in to get a better look.

The plans were wonky, to say the least. And rather ambitious. In Delaney's vision, the adjoining wall between the bakery and pizzeria had been removed. The alfresco dining area outside the pizzeria now took over the whole front of the bakery as well, blocking the current entrance door, which in the diagram had been turned into a window. The current bakery's kitchen had been completely stripped out, turned into the customer bathroom, while the pizzeria kitchen, double the size of the bakery's, was listed as the main one.

For some reason, Ali just could not envision Delaney's plan coming to life. It was a lot of work, and it created a large, unwieldy space, far from the cozy vibe she wanted to cultivate. In fact, it looked far more like a restaurant than a café, and Ali had learned the hard way that she and restaurants did not go well together. She'd never be able to forget how dreadful it had been working at *Eclairs* in LA, making nothing but crème brûlée for three long years. She'd also never be able to forget the moment she quit in a blaze of glory, making a huge public spectacle of herself in the process. But she held her tongue. She didn't want to hurt Delaney's feelings. Her friend had put in lots of effort to do this for her, for free, out of the kindness of her heart.

"Thanks for this," Ali told her friend. "I'll definitely consider it."

Delaney's brow twitched inwards. "Consider it? I — I thought you'd have more to say than that!"

Ali hesitated, feeling caught between a rock and a hard place. She'd never asked Delaney to make the plans, and she wasn't going to just go along with them for the sake of it. The pizzeria expansion was a huge deal. It needed to be perfect. She simply couldn't compromise just for the sake of being polite.

"I'm really impressed with what you've done," she said, choosing her words carefully. "But I don't want to rush into anything."

A look of hurt flashed across Delaney's eyes and Ali felt terrible for having caused it. She opened her mouth to offer more words of comfort and reassurance, but she didn't get a chance to because at that moment, something out the window drew her attention away.

A rotund man in a bright Hawaiian-print shirt and salmon-colored board shorts was heading in her direction. An untidy mass of strawberry blonde hair sitting atop a round, pink face confirmed her fear. It was Teddy.

Usually, Ali's heart soared at the sight of her brother, but today she was gripped by sudden anxiety. Teddy held a huge grudge against their father. If the two of them bumped into one another unexpectedly, there would be a huge dust-up.

"Piper, I need you to keep an eye on things for a second," Ali said, throwing off her apron and rushing out from behind the counter.

"Sure," Piper said with a small, perplexed frown.

Delaney put her hands on her hips and tracked Ali's trajectory across the bakery floor to the exit. "What about my plans?"

"We can talk about them later!"

"But where are you going?"

Ali reached the door and heaved it open. As she paused to call over her shoulder, Scruff zoomed straight through her legs. "I'll be back soon!" And with that, she raced outside into the sunshine, beelining for her brother so she could divert him before there was a catastrophe of epic proportions.

Teddy's strawberry blonde eyebrows drew together at the sight of her racing toward him.

"Morning!" she cried, forcing herself to sound cheery as she grabbed his arm and started to steer him down the boardwalk at speed in the opposite direction of the Willow Bay Inn where their father was staying.

Teddy frowned at her hand on his arm. "Erm... good morning...," he said, sounding perplexed. "Are you okay?"

"I'm fine!"

"Then why are you marching me along the boardwalk and away from the coffee?" He glanced mournfully back at the bakery where there was always a free caffeine fix waiting for him.

"I know a better place to get coffee," Ali exclaimed, far too enthusiastically.

"Better than the bakery? Really? Well, is it close? Because you know I'm not usually up this early and I won't be able to function until I've had it."

"Then you're in luck, because it's just here!" Ali gestured with her arms at one of the boardwalk's more generic coffee shops, one she had no real interest in trying.

"Here?" Teddy said with a grimace.

Ali tugged on his arm. "Yup! Come on! I can't wait to try it!"

But her tugging was useful. Teddy dug his heels in.

"What's going on?" he asked in a wary tone. "You're being weird. And why are you so manically happy?"

"I'm just happy to see you!" Ali cried. But then she halted. She was being ridiculous. It was better to come clean. Teddy would find out sooner or later, and it was better if he heard it from her.

She dropped the happy act and became immediately solemn. "You're right. I have something to tell you."

Teddy's whole demeanor immediately changed as he switched into his protective big brother role. He looped an arm over her shoulder and gave her a reassuring squeeze. "Then let's grab a coffee and talk."

Relieved, Ali felt herself relax into him. This was Teddy, her favorite person in the world. Of course, she could speak to him about her worries.

"Okay," she said, feeling a small weight lifted from her shoulder. "Just one request." She pulled a face at the coffeeshop in front of them. "We don't go there."

Teddy threw his head back and laughed. "Deal."

CHAPTER FOUR

Teddy placed two steaming cups of coffee on the table. The coffee shop that they'd chosen in the end was one of Willow Bay's newest, and was full of big, broad leafed, green potted plants. Gentle bossa nova music trilled in the background.

"Now, let me guess," Teddy said, taking his seat. "You're pregnant."

Ali rolled her eyes and pointed at the steaming mug of strong black coffee on the table between them. "Would I be drinking coffee if I was pregnant?" She shook her head. "No. It's not that."

Teddy stirred sugar into his coffee, glancing ahead ponderously. "Are you eloping?"

Ali couldn't help but scoff. Teddy knew full well how disastrous her love life had been recently. "And *who* would I be eloping with?"

"Nate."

"He's dating Carys now."

"Then Seth?"

Ali shook her head. "No. Not happening."

Teddy flashed her a knowing smirk. "Then how about *Detective Callihan...*"

At the mention of Detective Callihan, Ali felt a spark of excitement light inside of her and had to fight hard to stifle her smile. Sebastian Callihan was one of Willow Bay's detectives, and thanks to a series of bizarre murders over the last few months, Ali had had plenty of opportunities to get to know him. After the disaster of her long-term boyfriend Otis admitting he was gay, to a short-lived romance with surfer Nate, to an even shorter-lived romantic misunderstanding with hot dog seller Seth, it felt nice to have someone new to focus on. "How did you know?"

"About Detective Callihan?" Teddy replied, his eyes going wide. "I didn't! I was just teasing you, because he's so obviously into you. Ali, are you telling me you're into him too?"

Ali blushed as she realized she'd accidentally given the game away. "I guess. We went on a sort of date the other day. We just ran into each other at a festival on the beach. But he promised to ask me out on a real date sometime. And he's really smart, Teddy, and decent, and honest, and just a thoroughly good person. I mean I liked Nate and Seth too, but there's something different about Seb."

"I can tell," Teddy replied, his eyebrows up in astonishment. "So that's it then? That's your big news? You and *Seb* are becoming romantically entangled."

He clasped his hands together, fingers interlaced through each other as a visual demonstration, but Ali didn't reply, because she'd come back to reality with a bump.

She cupped her hands around the steaming coffee mug, letting the warmth comfort her. "No. It's something else."

Teddy must have noticed the change in her mood, because he reached out and patted her arm. "Whatever it is, you can tell me."

Ali peered up at her brother. The reappearance of their missing father was a huge deal, and not the sort of news that was easy to break, especially to the son who'd felt the most betrayed by him leaving in the first place. But Teddy needed to know, and so she found her courage and took a preparatory breath. "It's Dad..."

Teddy's expression remained the same, but behind his eyes, something shifted. "You found him?"

She nodded. "He's here."

"Here?"

"In Willow Bay."

Teddy sat back in his seat, eyebrows raised with shock. "Wow," he said, sounding astonished. "I don't know what to say."

It was a rare occurrence for Teddy to be lost for words, and Ali couldn't help but feel responsible. *She* was the one who'd wanted to reconnect with their father, after all. Teddy never asked for any of this; he was just being dragged along for the ride.

Ali reached out and took his hand. "I know it's a big shock. He got my note, the one I left for him in the desert, and drove here this morning. He's staying at the inn and— are you okay?"

Teddy seemed to be going red in the face, and he tugged at his shirt collar as if it was suddenly constricting him. "Yes. Yes. I'm fine. It's just...," he trailed off, his hesitancy making Ali's stomach swirl with dread. "It's just... I don't want to meet up with him." He shook his head to emphasize the point. "There's not going to be any father-son reunion. You know that, right?"

Now it was Ali's turn to be shocked. She'd been so wrapped up in her worries about breaking the news to Teddy, she hadn't actually considered what would happen once she did. It hadn't occurred to her that her brother would simply refuse to meet up with him. She had naively assumed if she ever *did* locate her dad, Teddy would change his mind.

"You don't?" she asked in a small, sad voice.

Teddy shook his head. "No. And I'm sorry. I don't want to hurt you, and I know you want some kind of happy family reunion, but I can't do it. At least not now. It would be too much upheaval. I have to stay focused on my movie."

At the mention of the independent movie Teddy had been cast in, Ali nodded. It made sense. After years as a struggling actor, the independent, gritty movie *Street Walkers* was about to become his big break, his first appearance on the silver screen. And though she wished the timing could align, she understood *why* Teddy didn't want to go there just yet. In many ways, she felt the same, didn't she? She was dreading "the talk" with Richard.

"It's alright," she told Teddy. "I understand the movie has to be your priority. I won't force anything on you."

Teddy nodded gratefully. "Good. Because that's why I came to see you in the first place." He smiled cheekily and reached into his bag, bringing out his cell phone. "I just got the editor's cut back!"

Ali faltered. Her brother had moved on from the topic of their absentee father so quickly it gave her whiplash. And while she respected Teddy's opinion not to meet with their father, she still would have appreciated the time to talk to him about it now and tell him how it was affecting her. Teddy had always been supportive, but now it felt like he was putting up a wall. She couldn't help but feel slightly dismissed.

"Look!" he said, turning the cell to face her and thrusting it beneath Ali's nose.

Ali had no choice but to push her emotions away and focus on her brother. This was his big moment, after all, and she wanted to support him even if he had failed to support her just now. So she took the phone and watched Teddy on the screen, his usual exuberant and flamboyant personality replaced with a dark, somber one, almost as if she was looking at a completely different person.

"This is amazing," Ali murmured. "You don't even look like you."

"I know," Teddy beamed. "Can you believe I'm going to be famous soon?" He raised his voice as he spoke, in a clear attempt to be overheard by the other people in the coffee shop. Ali cringed a little and handed him back the phone.

"Well, it looks great."

"Thanks," he replied, pocketing it.

27

Ali shifted in her seat. She really wanted to pick up the conversation about their dad again, but before she got a chance to speak, she was interrupted by Teddy's sudden excited gasp. She paused and frowned, then followed the direction of his gaze out the window of the pier-facing coffee shop they were in.

"I don't believe it!" Teddy exclaimed, his eyes going completely round. "Is that… is that…"

Ali craned her head, searching for whomever had caught Teddy's attention. It was probably someone famous. Teddy was an aspiring actor and seemed to possess an inbuilt honing instinct when it came to celebrities.

"Oh," he said, suddenly deflating. "No. I thought it was Tom Cruise. But it's just some guy with a metal detector." He paused and looked back at Ali. "Why *are* there so many people with metal detectors on the beach?"

"Someone found a gold coin. An antique. Now there's a rumor that there's more hidden treasure and all these weirdos with metal detecting machines have taken over the beach. There's even some TV show apparently coming to town."

"*Antiques Hunters?*" Teddy asked, looking excited. "With the guy? With the hair?" He did the same 1980's mullet mime with his hands that Piper had.

Ali smirked. "The very same."

"Oh wow!" Teddy cried. "We should hurry up with our coffees and get down to the beach in that case." Just like Piper, Teddy was like a moth to a flame for anything even remotely connected to celebrities, even Z-list ones with mullets presenting obscure antiques shows…

"Actually though," Ali said, twiddling the handle of her coffee mug. "Before you rush off, I do need to speak to you about something—"

She paused, interrupted by the sound of Teddy thudding his coffee mug down. He'd drained it in two seconds flat, knocking it back like a shot, and was now standing up. He ushered her to do the same with his hands in an impatient gesture, his gaze still fixed out the window. "Come on, sis. Drink up, drink up. Opportunities don't come knocking every day. You have to seize them when they present themselves."

Ali sighed and relented. She downed the rest of her coffee and stood, dropping a tip onto the tabletop before following Teddy out of the coffee shop onto the boardwalk.

As she followed Teddy along the palm-tree lined boardwalk, Ali realized just how crazy busy it was on the beach that morning. She'd been so focused on the other matter she hadn't really been paying attention to her surroundings, but now she could see there were significantly more people than had been there when she arrived at work.

Just then, Scruff came racing up behind them, wagging his tail and barking excitedly.

"There you are," Ali said, reaching down to pet him. "I wondered where you'd got to."

He barked eagerly, and there was an enthusiastic sparkle in his eyes, like he wanted to share something with her.

"What is it?" Ali asked, standing up.

Sure enough, Scruff started heading along the boardwalk, the opposite direction Teddy wanted to go.

"Hey," Teddy said. "Where are you going?"

"I think Scruff wants to show me something," Ali said over her shoulder, as she kept her gaze on the little pup winding his way through the legs of the increasingly busy throng of people.

"But what about mullet man?" Teddy pouted.

"I'm sure he'll be there when we get back," Ali replied, before facing her brother. "Unless that's what Scruff wants to show us..."

She didn't need to say any more. Teddy diverted his course and followed.

They followed Scruff as he weaved his way through the crowd and found themselves standing outside an enormous boutique pet store.

"That's it?" Teddy said, unimpressed. "A pet store?"

It was a new store to the boardwalk, a high-end pet fashion boutique and supply store and by the looks of things it was in the midst of its grand opening. There were balloons out front, and loud music pumping through speakers. A bubble machine was on full blast, too, and there was an inflatable dog by the door.

Scruff started barking at it, bouncing from foot to foot in front of it.

"I see," Ali said with a chuckle. "That's what Scruff wanted to show me. He's made a friend."

Teddy laughed. "A friend or an enemy? I can't quite tell."

Scruffy was going slightly crazy at the inflatable dog making very strange, un-dog-like movements as it bobbed and floated around in the breeze. It was clearly blowing his little mind.

Just then, a woman came out of the store with a mass of glossy auburn hair reaching down to her waist. She had a name tag on. Shauna. She must be the owner, Ali thought, and she watched as the woman stood with her hands on her hips glaring at the beach.

Ali decided to introduce herself to her new neighbor. "Hi. I'm Ali. I own the bakery along the boardwalk. Are you new?"

"Yes," the woman replied. "Is it always like this?"

Ali shook her head. "No, the beach isn't usually full of people with metal detectors. Someone found a rare gold coin and now everyone thinks there's treasure. There's also a TV show coming to town to film it."

"Perfect," the woman said with wry sarcasm. "Just what I need on my grand opening day. More competition for attention." She huffed and her frown deepened.

It appeared Shauna was just as unenthusiastic as Ali was when it came to the TV types and day trippers who descended upon the town causing nothing but commotion in their wake. Perhaps Ali had found a kindred spirit in her new boardwalk neighbor?

"Bad timing," Ali said, sympathetically. "Don't worry. I'm sure among the crowds some of them must have pets?" Although if the rest were anything like the conspiracy theorist man who'd been disgusted by Scruff, then probably not.

The woman remained unsmiling. "You think?" she said sarcastically, in a tone that rubbed Ali, who was just trying to be nice, the wrong way. "I'm sure plenty of them have pets. But they're from out of town. No one buys pet supplies if they have to travel halfway across the country to get them home. No one is going to buy one of my cat climbing gyms, are they? And I doubt any of them brought their dogs or horses with them for my special grooming services." She was getting quite irate now. "I mean how long are they even going to be here for? When are they leaving? How long before it all goes back to normal?"

Ali raised her eyebrows. Shauna seemed to be rather highly strung, and far from the kindred spirit Ali had first thought she may be.

"Well, when it comes to Willow Bay, there isn't really such a thing as normal," she said. "If it's not TV shows it's hot dog eating contests. There's always something crazy going on here."

Shauna rolled her eyes. "Great," she muttered sarcastically, then she turned on the spot and marched back into her store.

Ali exchanged a look with Teddy. "I think she might be regretting moving to Willow Bay."

Teddy chuckled. "You think?" he said, mimicking the same sarcastic sneer Shauna had used.

Ali couldn't help but giggle. Her brother's impressions were spot on.

"Oh shoot," Teddy said, suddenly, looking down at his flashing cell phone. "I have to go. Meeting with the agent." He hurriedly kissed her cheek, then turned away and pressed his cell phone to his ear, hurrying off before Ali even had a chance to say goodbye.

She watched him disappear in one direction, then looked back in the other, toward her bakery, and the meeting with her father she was dreading. She swallowed the lump of anxiety in her throat and headed off.

But as she got within eyesight of the bakery, Ali was confronted by a sight she never expected to see. It was not her father arriving for their planned meeting, but a long line stretching all the way out of the bakery door and along the boardwalk. A long line filled with yet more treasure hunters, all looking flustered as if they were melting beneath the hot Calfornia sun.

"Oh boy," Ali said, putting on her game face. "Things are about to get interesting."

CHAPTER FIVE

'I guess even treasure hunters get hungry...,' Ali thought as she marched toward the bakery, passing along the long line of strange people holding metal detectors.

"Hey! Lady!" an angry voice shouted from the line. "No cutting!"

Ali turned back and pointed at her *Seaside Sweets* T-shirt. "Don't worry," she said, brightly. "I work here!"

"About time!" the angry man shouted back. "I've been waiting in line for forever!"

Ali rushed past the rude man and went inside, rushing straight for the counter.

At the sight of her, Piper's deer-in-the-headlights look immediately turned to relief. "Ali! Thank goodness you're back! They started arriving by the bus load! Literally! And they all want coffee!"

She seemed to be on the verge of a nervous breakdown, and Ali rushed around the counter to join her. She grabbed her apron from the hooks and threw it on, then dashed to the coffee machine which was hissing in the corner like an angry cobra. The poor thing was a mess, with coffee splattered all over it and discarded espresso cups lying haphazardly on the counter around it. Ali quickly grabbed the black Americano that was sitting there and jammed a lid on top, whirling around to address the crowd.

"Who ordered black Americano?" she called to the waiting rabble.

"I did!" about five different voices said in unison, and a bunch of different people started elbowing their way toward the front counter.

Ali flashed Piper a glance. "Which one of them ordered first?"

"I don't know!" Piper cried. She hurriedly pointed to a man in a slogan shirt that read: *NYC Detectorists' Club*. "I think it was him."

The man next to him glowered and balled his fists. "No way! *I* was first!" He was also in a slogan shirt, this one reading: *Toronto Treasure Hunter's Society*. Had people really traveled so far just for the chance to find a gold coin on a beach, Ali wondered?

"Don't worry, sir," Ali said to the Toronto Treasure hunter as she handed the NYC treasure hunter the coffee. "Yours will be ready in thirty seconds!"

"Thirty seconds can be the difference between leaving here empty handed or leaving here with untold wealth," the Toronto man said, as he flashed the stink eye at the smug looking NYC man.

Ali was tempted to ask him why he'd stopped for a coffee in the first place if time was so precious, but she held her tongue, because if there was one thing she'd learned from her days at *Eclairs* (beyond how to make crème brûlée, of course), it was that the customer was always right.

She turned back to the coffee machine and filled it up with fresh beans. "Has it been this busy all morning?" she asked Piper over her shoulder.

"Yes!" Piper exclaimed, wiping the perspiration from her forehead. "Pretty much as soon as you ran away to do your errand, they mobbed us. I don't even know what happened to Delaney. I can only hope she got out alive."

It was the typical hyperbole Ali had come to expect from Piper, but she did feel bad about the way she'd run off to speak to Teddy. Especially when Piper still didn't know what was going on with her father. And now with the onslaught of treasurer hunters descending on the town from every far-flung place imaginable, she was very unlikely to get a chance to tell her. But her father was also very unlikely to even get inside the store with the caffeine desperate crowds clamoring like zombies for blood, and Ali had to admit she was secretly relieved for the distraction.

"Well, it looks like you've done a great job keeping them fed and watered," she continued, as she poured two Americanos into takeout cups with practiced elegance. She turned back to the counter, handing the Toronto man his cup well within her promised thirty-seconds. "And we're not out of stock yet, so that's a plus." She looked up at the crowds and held the second takeout cup aloft. "I've got another black Americano!" The crowds scrambled.

Piper handed a brown paper bag filled with cookies over the counter to a woman waiting on the other side in a bright red *Delaware Detectorists' Do It Best* shirt. "You say that, but they've had some very unusual requests. And I've had to turn quite a few of them away."

"Unusual how?" Ali asked.

But Piper didn't need to answer, because at that moment a young slim man stepped up to the counter wearing a t-shirt that said: *The Aliens Walk Among Us* and an aluminum tin hat with what appeared to be a radio antenna stuck on it. Ali widened her eyes, and she thought back to the gruff guy who'd snapped at Scruff earlier that morning. Perhaps this was one of his friends?

"See what I mean?" Piper said out the side of her mouth.

Ali gave her a subtle nod, then smiled her most affable smile at the strange young man. "Welcome to *Seaside Sweets*. Can I help you?"

"Do you serve coffee?" the man barked.

"Yes we do."

"Do you serve it in aluminum cups?"

"No, we serve it in paper cups," Ali replied in her calmest customer service voice, before adding silently in her mind, *'Like normal people.'*

The young man stared at her like *she* was the weird one. "Huh," he scoffed. "When will you people ever learn? Aluminum is the only thing that blocks them from reading your thoughts. When they arrive and are able to construct a perfect replica of you from your memories, you'll really be sorry." Then he turned, looking disappointed and shaking his head as he trudged glumly out of the store.

Ali side-eyed Piper. Piper flashed her a *see-what-I-mean* look.

The bell over the door tinkled nonstop as more of the bizarre treasure hunters came in. The next group appeared to be pagans or shamans, dressed in robes and carrying dowsing rods rather than metal detectors.

It felt to Ali like things were descending into chaos. The store was becoming more and more crowded as more and more quirky treasure hunters entered. Ali really hoped her dad didn't pick this moment to arrive. He'd get the wrong impression of her store if he walked in now while it was full of this strange bunch of treasure hunters!

Suddenly, someone sitting in the window stood up and exclaimed, "They're here!"

After her run in with two alien-enthusiasts, Ali's mind turned immediately to spaceships and little green men. But instead, she saw what appeared to be a large white television crew truck rolling along the boardwalk. *Antiques Hunters* had arrived...

Everyone who'd been waiting to be served abandoned the line, rushing for the window, chattering excitedly as they craned to get a glimpse of their favorite Z-lister. Ali was about to say something to Piper about it but discovered her assistant had already abandoned her post behind the counter and was rushing across the bakery floor to the window to join them.

"They're here!" Piper cried, glancing back over her shoulder at Ali. "Can I go? Can I?" She was already removing her apron.

"Yes, okay," Ali said, feeling like an out of touch mother taking her young daughter to see her favorite pop group.

Piper squealed and rushed out of the exit along with the other treasure hunters, who were filing out of the bakery like someone had pulled the bath plug. Within five minutes flat, Ali was standing alone in the bakery which looked like a bomb had hit the place. She was about to reach for the mop to start tidying up but was overcome with curiosity. What was it about this show everyone loved so much?

As a naturally inquisitive person, Ali simply couldn't just let it be, and decided it wouldn't hurt to take a peek, especially since it looked like no one would be coming in for a while.

"The cleaning can wait," Ali said, as if excusing herself aloud, then she hurried out the bakery, locking the door behind her, and ran off to see what all the fuss was about.

CHAPTER SIX

Quite the crowd had formed on the beach by the time Ali arrived. She stood on her tiptoes, craning to see over the heads of the people, since her short stature always put her at such a disadvantage when it came to crowds.

Finally, a gap emerged in the group, and Ali got her first glimpse of the source of everyone's interest: a man with an '80s mullet.

'So this must be the presenter,' Ali thought, remembering the man both Piper and Teddy had told (and mimed to) her about! He was marching down the sand toward the shoreline, talking into a comically oversized orange microphone in a zealous manner while glancing periodically behind at the camera operator following him. The man appeared to be struggling to keep his balance with the large, cumbersome camera on his shoulder while staggering on the uneven sand.

'What kind of show is *this?'* Ali thought wryly, walking alongside the rest of the audience as they followed excitedly after Mullet Man.

With a name like *Antiques Hunters,* Ali had been expecting the presenter to be some kind of well-to-do man in a tweed coat. With a monocle. Perhaps even a pair of fluffy white mutton chops thrown in for good measure. Instead, she'd found a loud man with a zany haircut and silly microphone who looked more like he belonged on a kid's TV show than an antiques one.

She'd also been expecting the show to be stationary, perhaps involving a set consisting of a comfy armchair and grand wooden table, set up on the beach with the ocean behind. Instead, the show seemed to involve a lot of racing around, and the poor cameraman was bright red as he lugged his heavy equipment down the beach, huffing and puffing to keep up with the presenter as if he was filming a real lifeguard beach rescue show rather than an antiques one.

'Well, Piper did say it wasn't a usual antiques show...,' Ali thought.

The presenter made it to the shore where the beach-goer who'd found the gold coin that morning was waiting for him.

"And here's the man of the hour! It's Vincent Cole. Vinnie, how are you feeling?" He shoved the microphone under the beach-goer's nose.

"I'm feeling fantastic," Vincent said, beaming widely into the camera which had finally caught up to them. He was quite the showman and was thoroughly lapping up the attention. "But I'll be feeling even more fantastic when you tell me how much my treasure is worth."

The presenter laughed. "I'm sure you will! But first, can you show our viewers at home what you found?"

"Of course." Vincent pulled the gold coin from his pocket and showed it to the camera, then to the crowd arcing around him. They let out a collective "oooh." Even Ali had to admit to herself that there was something romantic about the ancient gold coin washing up on the shoreline of her little beach town.

"And you found it right here?" Mullet Man continued, prodding the big orange microphone at Vincent's face.

"Right here!" Vincent exclaimed with a big, wide grin, pointing to the sand beneath his feet.

Mullet Man nodded with exaggerated enthusiasm. "Well, I think it's about time we found out what your treasure is worth. Which means it's time to bring out…"

The crowd joined in with him, chanting, "Eddie Expert!" in unison. Ali raised her eyebrows and glanced around, feeling like the odd one out in a crowd of uber fans.

Just then, the crowds parted and from them emerged a nerdy looking man in a tweed jacket and monocle. Ali started to laugh. It was almost as if she'd manifested the man with her mind!

The audience clapped as Eddie Expert took his position beside Vincent. He seemed timid, his demeanor far less gung-ho than Mullet Man. He even blushed as the big orange microphone was shoved his way.

"So tell us, Eddie," Mullet Man said in his loud, brash, children's TV presenter voice. "What do we have here?"

Eddie held his hand out to Vincent and, after pausing for a moment as if reluctant to let it out of his possession, Vincent placed the coin in his palm.

Silence fell as Eddie began inspecting the coin through his monocle. Ali suspected the monocle was just a prop, and this was all showmanship for the sake of the cameras. Showmanship that Eddie probably wished he didn't have to take part in; his cheeks were practically crimson now with the crowd on tenterhooks and all eyes on him.

"Well, it's a Spanish coin," he began, his voice unsteady. "Better known as a doubloon. You can see here from the uneven edges that it was made through a hammering process, rather than a press, which would date it to the fifteen-hundreds."

"The fifteen-hundreds!" Mullet Man repeated, but in a tone that implied this was the most fascinating thing in the world, in case it was lost on anyone. The crowd dutifully gasped.

"Yes, yes, but what's it *worth?*" Vincent asked impatiently.

Eddie Expert looked flustered at the interruption, and stammered, before finding his place again. "Right. Yes. As I was saying, hammered coins are rare. Which makes them more valuable. A coin like this, in this condition, very likely ended up here from a shipwreck. Possibly even a pirate wreck, having been stolen during its transportation overseas from the Spanish mint. Something like this will be exceedingly valuable at auction."

"*How* valuable?" Vincent demanded, and Ali couldn't help but notice the way his eyes were bulging like Golem's.

"Well, it's hard to say exactly," Eddie Expert continued. "But I would suspect several thousand dollars."

"*Thou— thousand?*" Vincent replied, stammering breathlessly.

Mullet Man jumped in, waving his big orange microphone like a beacon. "You heard it here first folks! There's treasure on this very beach worth thousands of dollars! How much more do you think there is, Eddie?"

Eddie rubbed his gray tufts of hair nervously. "Well… I mean… it's impossible to know for sure if there even is anything—"

Mullet Man cut him off mid-sentence. "But if it came off a shipwreck there *must* be! Right? Right?"

He was goading the poor man, and Eddie Expert relented with an uncertain sounding, "Yes. Probably. I suspect. Maybe…"

That was all it took. A vague promise of untold riches sent the crowd into an eruption of cheers and claps, before they darted away, scrambling feverishly to find their own gold coin. Within seconds, people were crouching in the sand digging with their hands. Meanwhile, the strange group of detectorists who'd been in the bakery moments earlier started descending on the beach at speed, their machines crackling as they started scanning for treasure. Vincent looked flummoxed and he went off after them, elbows protruding. The poor, exhausted looking cameraman followed, lugging his heavy equipment as sweat rolled down his back.

Ali was the only person that didn't hurry off in search of gold. She stayed where she was, more intrigued by the *Antiques Hunters* crew than the treasure. Because the moment the camera had stopped rolling, Mullet Man's goofy persona had disappeared, so quickly it was as if a switch had been flicked off.

He lowered his microphone and addressed a woman standing nearby with a headset and clipboard. "Where's the toilet? I'm about to pee myself here."

His voice was gruff now, abrupt and unenthusiastic. It was as if his TV persona had been extinguished like candle flame.

The clipboard woman pointed behind her. "We're setting up all the amenities over there, on the boardwalk."

Ali glanced behind to see that in the short time she'd been on the beach, a big white TV van had parked on the boardwalk alcove directly in front of the bakery. Several crew members were putting up a large white tent and a forklift truck was currently reversing a row of porta potties into position... right outside the bakery door!

"No!" Ali cried with despair. They would totally obstruct the view of the bakery from the boardwalk and beach, which would directly impact how much foot traffic she got. Not to mention it was totally gross!

"Give them five minutes," the clipboard lady continued to mullet man. "The water tanks need to be filled before you do your business."

Ali grimaced with disgust. She couldn't let this happen!

She marched toward the woman with the clipboard, who'd already turned away and started heading up the beach.

"Excuse me!" she cried, hurrying her step to keep up. "Excuse me? Are you running this thing?"

As Ali ran alongside her, the woman turned to face her. She had a very judgmental expression on her face, with her long, thin nose lifted to the air in disdain. "Pardon?"

Ali quickened her steps to keep pace. "I asked if you're running this thing."

She stopped abruptly and spoke in a haughty manner. "If by *thing* you mean the number one antiques show on Channel 9, then yes. I am." She looked down her nose at Ali. "Why? What's your problem?"

Ali pointed up the beach to the boardwalk, where the porta potties were now in position. "My bakery is there. And you can't put a load of porta potties in front of it! I didn't sign anything to say you could!"

The woman's dark eyes narrowed. Then an expression Ali couldn't place flashed behind them, and she grabbed her radio. As she brought it up to her lips, Ali presumed she was about to call back the driver of the forklift and get him to move the potties to a more conspicuous location. But instead, she smiled a thin-lipped, malevolent smile, pressed down the button and said, "Jack, get the camera back up here. A situation is kicking off."

With a frown of bemusement, Ali watched as the cameraman turned away from a group of bikini-wearing women using a pink frisbee to dig in the sand and hurried back along the beach toward her. As he passed, groups of diggers stopped what they were doing and followed him.

Mullet Man sighed wearily, shook his shoulders and heaved up his orange microphone. Then suddenly, he grinned at Ali and his TV persona was back in full, disconcerting force.

"Ladies and gents at home," he announced into the microphone. "We have a situation kicking off here at Willow Bay beach!"

"Kicking off?" Ali said, putting her hands on her hips as the orange microphone appeared under her nose. She thwacked it away. "I'm not kicking off!"

Just then, Jack the camera man arrived, wheezing and panting as he shoved his camera toward her. A group of onlookers crowded in, craning to see what was causing the kerfuffle. Ali took a step back, frowning at the intrusion of privacy.

"Can you stop doing that please?" she demanded, testily. "I'm simply saying that you can't put a porta potty outside my bakery without getting permission."

Mullet Man kept shoving his microphone at her face, while Jack the cameraman wheezed like a pug and wiped sweat from his face. All the while, the woman with the clipboard grinned greedily at the unfolding drama for her precious TV show.

"Can you please stop shoving that thing at me?" Ali exclaimed, feeling goaded by their behavior.

More onlookers were noticing the commotion now and were stopping what they were doing to come over and gawk. Ali started to feel even more self-conscious.

"Ugh, I know her," a voice said.

Ali looked up to see Vincent Cole, the beach goer who'd found the coin and started this whole thing. He had his hands on his hips and glowered at her.

"She's a loser wannabe," he continued, rolling his eyes. "The town's drama queen who's always trying to muscle in on everyone else's business."

Ali gasped with offense. The woman with the clipboard's eyes flashed with malevolent glee.

Ali turned to Vincent and frowned. "Excuse me? I don't even know you."

"No, but I know you. Unfortunately." He fixed his glower on her. "And I know you simply can't stand the attention being on anyone but you!" His tone turned catty. "Sorry sweetie, but for once you're not the center of attention. No one cares about you. All eyes are on me right now. So why don't you run along to your pathetic little bakery, you sad little wannabe?"

"I'm not a wannabe!" Ali cried, insulted by his harsh words, however incorrect they may be. "And I'm certainly not looking for attention. I couldn't care less about your stupid coin. If anyone should leave, it's you! Or maybe I should throw your precious gold coin in the ocean?"

The crowd gasped and giggled, equal parts shocked and titillated by the unfolding drama. The woman with the clipboard looked thrilled by the unfolding events, which were being captured diligently by Jack the sweaty cameraman and further goaded by the presenter with the mullet.

"What do you say to that, Vinnie?" he said, nudging the angry man with the microphone. "This crazy lady wants to throw your coin in the ocean!"

Ali groaned with humiliation. She'd played right into their hands by losing her temper…

Realizing she'd taken things too far, Ali decided the only damage control available to her now was to make a swift exit. So she turned on the spot and muscled her way through the crowd, desperate to retreat to the safety of her bakery.

But she'd not made it ten paces when her attention was drawn to someone in the crowd. One of the onlookers who'd been watching her this whole time.

Her stomach dropped to her toes. It was her dad, and he'd witnessed it all.

41

CHAPTER SEVEN

Feeling mortified by what had happened on the beach, Ali slumped into the window seat of the bakery and buried her face in her hands. It just wasn't like her to lose her temper or make a spectacle like that. It was like her infamous crème brûlée outburst at *Eclairs* all over again. It must be all the emotional stress from her dad reappearing, not to mention the way the camera crew had goaded her, and Vincent had insulted her. Everything had boiled over, making her behave in a manner that made her toes curl as she replayed it in her mind.

Her father took a seat at the table opposite her and she peeped through her fingers at him. She didn't even dare wonder what he was thinking of her. He was probably regretting coming here and getting back in touch with her.

"I'm so embarrassed," she muttered.

But to her surprise, her father reached across the table and patted her arm. "Don't be."

"I'm not usually like that," she added.

"You must have inherited your temper from me."

Ali tensed. Though she'd appreciated his attempt to comfort her, something about the comment chafed. It was the suggestion she'd inherited anything from the man who'd been largely absent during her formative years.

"Thanks," she muttered, sliding her arm out from under his hand.

Silence fell. They were the only people in the bakery. The usual customers were either staying away because of her angry outburst or because of the proximity of the porta potties. Either way, her usually bustling store was empty, and it only made Ali feel even worse.

"People are fickle," Richard continued, clearly not reading the room. "Everyone will forget about it and move onto the next drama before you even know it." He patted her hand, *again,* even though he had to lean across the table to reach it this time. "Cheer up, chicken."

'Oh no...,' Ali thought. Now he was bringing in pet names? She was so far from being comfortable with that, and she bristled even more.

"If you think people will forget about it and move on, then you don't know the people of Willow Bay," she told him. "I do. They'll

42

never let me live it down. Knowing my luck, someone probably filmed the whole thing and has already uploaded it."

She reached into her pocket for her cell phone, but Richard stopped her with a hand on her arm. She halted and looked up to see him regarding her with a serious expression. Ali instantly knew why he'd turned so somber. He wanted to have "the talk."

Her heart began to race. The moment she'd been anxiously anticipating had arrived. But the timing couldn't be worse. The argument with Vincent on the beach had made her feel fragile; anything her father said now had the capacity to shatter her.

"Dad... you don't need to..."

But before Richard had a chance to speak, a loud tinkle sounded out. Ali's eyes darted over his shoulder to the bakery door and she sighed with relief as Piper came waltzing in for her check-in.

"Hey, Ali, you should see what's going on down the beach!" she exclaimed animatedly. "Someone found another gold coin, but then someone else claimed he found it first, and they started fighting each other! With fists!" She started punching the air in mimicry. "But then it turned out not to be an antique gold coin at all! It was just some European coin one of the tourists had dropped! The *Antiques Hunters* team caught the whole thing on camera and I'm pretty sure I got into the background of every shot." She grinned and let out a squeal of joy. "I'm going to be on TV!"

When she finally reached the end of her monologue, she took in a big breath of air and looked at Ali expectantly. Clearly, she was waiting for some kind of celebration from Ali. When none came, her blonde brows drew together and her prehnite green eyes began to dart back and forth between Ali and her father. Ali gave her a look, trying to silently communicate the situation to her.

At last, it seemed to dawn on Piper what was happening, and she took an exaggerated step back as if in surprise. "Woah, Ali," she said, shaking her head. "This guy looks just like you!"

Ali couldn't help but cringe. Piper had charged in like a bull in a china shop interrupting the long-anticipated moment with her father, and she'd *still* not put two and two together. "That's because it's my father," Ali explained.

Piper gasped. "Oh! Oh my gosh! No way! But you never told me your dad was in town."

"I never got the chance," Ali replied.

"It's a surprise visit," Richard added. He stood from his chair and offered his hand out to her to shake. Ali couldn't help but notice how much less awkward he was around Piper than he'd been around her. "I'm Richard," he said. "Ali's dad."

Piper took his hand and did a little curtsy. "I'm Piper, Ali's clumsy assistant. But I'm sure she's told you all about me!"

She giggled but Ali tensed at the faux pas. Of course, she'd not told her father about her, she hadn't had the chance to tell him about anything...

An awkward silence fell, all three averting each other's eyes.

Evidently uncomfortable, Piper coughed into her fist. "So, I'm just going to do a wipe down of the kitchen...," she mumbled, before scurrying away through the steel swing doors and out of sight.

As soon as the doors stopped flapping, Richard turned to Ali. The same serious somber look had returned to his eyes that had been there before Piper burst in, the one that told Ali he wanted to have the talk.

"Can we go somewhere private?" he asked. "Somewhere we can have a proper chat?"

Ali immediately felt a headache coming on and started rubbing between her eyes. "I can't," she said. "Piper's not really working today and with only me on shift, I'll need to stay on site."

Richard looked around at the otherwise empty bakery. "Well, I suppose if Piper's heading out anyway, and everyone else is busy down on the beach, it will be quiet enough for us to talk here."

Ali floundered. She just didn't feel ready for this. It had all been sprung on her so suddenly, and though there were questions burning in her mind, she also felt like there was a huge wall blocking her from asking them, like her tongue was tied.

"This morning is kind of busy with other stuff. I need to look at the expansion plans for the pizzeria and make some calls."

"You've had plans drawn up?" Richard asked, brightening immediately. "Let me take a look. I could save you some effort and money!"

Ali looked at him with uncertainty. "How?"

"Because I have a degree in architecture," he said. "Remember?"

Ali gasped. She had completely forgotten, and she felt incredibly guilty that her treacherous brain had decided such a piece of information wasn't worth holding on to. But after sixteen years without seeing her dad, forgetting key details about him was to be expected, wasn't it?

"I'm sorry, it slipped my mind," she said in an apologetic voice.

Richard nodded, looking lackluster.

Ali felt a desperate need to fix the situation. "Yes!" she blurted.

He frowned. "Yes?"

"To looking at the expansion plans," Ali said. "I'd really like your help. My friend drew them as a favor but they're not really what I had in mind. And she's not a professional. She runs a craft store. Shall I fetch them? And a couple of coffees? Do you drink coffee?"

Richard nodded and smiled. "That sounds good."

Ali sighed with relief and hurried off to collect the coffee and plans so they could get to work.

*

With next to no customers coming in, and with her dad's expert help, Ali was able to make quite a bit of headway with the expansion plans. By the end of the day, she had drawn up a fully-fledged diagram that was far more closely aligned with her own vision than Delaney's. *And* it wasn't a wonky drawing done in colored pencils, but an exact one made with a ruler and protractor and all the correct measurements.

When the clock hit five, Ali actually felt a little disappointed that it had ended. With a practical task to focus on, Ali had been far more comfortable in her dad's company. In fact, she'd actually enjoyed spending time with him. He hadn't tried to have any deep, heavy conversations with her all day, and Ali had been grateful for the break. It was just a shame about those porta potties...

"So?" Richard said as he followed her out of the store into the warm evening. "Shall we grab some dinner?"

Ali paused mid-way through locking the door and glanced over his shoulder. There was that look again. That serious, somber look. She felt herself freeze up.

"Tonight?" she said, evasively. "I can't. I have a prior engagement I can't get out of."

Richard looked immediately disappointed, and Ali felt terrible.

"But how about you come to the bakery tomorrow?" she added quickly. "We could hang out again while I work? I mean, Piper will be following the camera crew around again, and I really enjoyed the company..." She trailed off, feeling her cheeks growing warm.

"As long as I'm not in the way," Richard said.

"You're not," Ali said, hurriedly. "We could look at the plans some more. Maybe look into some contractors? Make some calls?"

A small smile flickered at the sides of Richard's lips, and the sadness in his eyes lifted. "I'd like that. That would be nice."

"Then it's a date," Ali said, grinning.

"Okay. See you tomorrow," Richard smiled in return and waved as he headed away into the warm evening.

With a heavy sigh, Ali turned back to the store and locked it securely. She knew she was just delaying the inevitable when it came to the heart to heart with her father, but something inside of her was telling her it was the right thing to do. She'd *enjoyed* her day with him. She hadn't felt bad, or nervous, or any sense of dread and doom. It had felt good, and nice, and altogether healing. Why would she let something like the pesky truth ruin all that? Couldn't she allow herself just a few days of blissful ignorance before reality hit?

Just then, she heard a bark and turned to see Scruff come racing toward her.

"Hey, Lil' Dude," she said, crouching down for the usual ear scritches.

But rather than stopping, Scruff passed her, barking as he went.

Ali frowned with confusion and watched as Scruff stopped a few paces from her, looked back, barked, then repeated the process. Ali had never seen Scruff behave that way before, but she got the distinct impression he was trying to get her to follow him. He appeared to be heading toward the beach, taking a few paces in that direction before turning back and letting out several insistent barks.

A strange feeling of anxiety came over Ali as she followed after him.

As soon as she began following, Scruff quickened his pace. Soon, Ali was jogging to keep up with him as he carried on his routine — barking, pausing, looking over his shoulder to make sure she was still there, then resuming running.

"Where is he taking me?" Ali said aloud, as she noticed they were coming up to the pier.

Then suddenly, she could no longer see Scruff, and she realized he'd disappeared into the small space between the boardwalk and the sand.

She shuddered. She did not want to go in there. There wasn't enough room to stand upright, and it was dark and creepy. But Scruff was barking more and more insistently so Ali fought her instincts to run away and ducked her head down.

At first, she saw nothing. But as her eyes adjusted to the gloom, she realized there was something there. A long, dark shape.

She gasped. Was it a person?

"Hello?" she called. "Are you okay? Are you hurt?"

There was no reply. She inched closer, straining to hear whether the person was breathing or not, or if they were emitting any sounds of distress. But they were silent, and it was too dark to see whether their chest was rising or falling.

A terrible sense of dread washed over Ali as she took yet another step into the dank space, closer to the figure.

"Hello? Are you okay? Do you need help?"

She reached out with a shaking hand and tapped the person on the shoulder. Nothing happened. She tried again, harder this time, more insistent. Again, the figure simply lay still and silent.

"I'm going to try and help you, okay?" Ali said, and this time she took the figure by the shoulders and heaved them toward her.

The figure was far heavier than she'd been expecting, and she had to put a lot of effort into rolling them toward her. The sand was slippery beneath her feet, making it hard to find purchase.

With a final grunt of effort, Ali pulled the person as hard as she could toward her. Suddenly, they rolled in one fast motion to face her; and Ali fell back onto her behind in the sand.

"Oof," she cried as she righted herself.

But as she looked back up at the person under the boardwalk, she knew instantly the man was dead. His arm had flopped out during the roll and lay out of the shadows on the sand in a beam of light. His skin was completely white.

Ali screamed and scrambled back, kicking sand with her sneakers in her haste to get away.

That's when she realized she knew the face staring unseeingly through her. It was Vincent Cole. The man who'd found the first gold coin. He'd been stabbed.

CHAPTER EIGHT

Ali sat on the sand, her knees to her chest, her arms wrapped tightly around them, rocking back and forth as she stared at Vincent Cole's dead body. She felt frozen. Numb. So shocked by the sight of the dead man that she couldn't even move.

Coming from somewhere not too far away, Ali heard a bark. Before she even had time to register what was happening, Scruff was right there, racing around her in circles with his brown eyes fixed intently on her as he barked and kicked up sand beneath his paws.

Ali shifted, moving her cramped legs into a crossed-leg position. Scruff bounded straight into her lap and pawed at her shirt with a concerned whine. He left streaks of sand all down the front of her shirt, but at last, his efforts paid off, and Ali was snapped out of her trance. She enclosed her arms around the little dog and buried her face into the scraggly fur on his flank, feeling grounded and comforted by his warm presence.

"Oh Scruff," she murmured to him. "I can't believe this. It's terrible. Awful."

Scruff whined sadly and began to lick her face with tender care. It was only then that Ali realized there were tear tracks running down her cheeks. She'd been in such a state of shock, she hadn't even noticed she'd started crying. How long had she been in her daze for? How long had she been sitting here in the sand, silently crying while staring numbly at the dead body in the shadowy space beneath the boardwalk?

Suddenly, reality struck so fast it gave her whiplash. It felt like a blindfold had been pulled away from her eyes, or like she'd suddenly bumped back to Earth from a state of zero-gravity. And as the veil of shock evaporated, a stark reality was left in its place, a terrifying reality that brought with it an overwhelming sense of terrible doom.

Vincent Cole was dead. Murdered. And she was the only person in the world who knew.

"I need to call the cops!" she cried, the feeling of responsibility hitting her like a gale force wind.

She scooched Scruff off her lap and with shaking hands reached into her pocket. She managed to inch her cell phone out, then held it in her trembling hands, staring at it briefly with confusion as if she'd forgotten how to operate it. She shook herself. "Focus, Ali. Focus."

She keyed in the number and dialed the station.

"Willow Bay police," a woman's voice said in her ear. "What is the nature of your emergency?"

Ali's gaze automatically fell to the knife lying in the sand. It was an unusual design, a fold-out blade with a couple of attachments, similar to an army knife but much bigger. The handle seemed to be made of a heavy, solid wood, and it was curved as if to comfortably fit the grip of the user.

"There's been a murder," she said.

"A murder?" the woman repeated in her ear. "What makes you think there's been a murder?"

Ali got the distinct impression from her tone that she thought she was dealing with a crank call, so she spoke in the most clear, determined, no-nonsense voice she could muster. "Because I'm looking at a man's dead body and there's a weapon lying next to him."

"Where are you, ma'am?" the voice in her ear said.

Ali glanced ahead at the shadowy space beneath the boardwalk. It was too vague a location. She looked behind her at the crisscrossing wooden pillars that made up the under-structure of the pier, where the dark wood was speckled with mildew and barnacles. "I'm on the beach. Beneath the pier."

Her voice quivered as she spoke, and it sounded as if it was coming from a great distance away. Scruff turned in anxious circles in front of her, clearly perturbed by the whole thing. He wasn't used to seeing or hearing her like this. She reached out to soothe him, twiddling her fingers through his fur the way she would if they were just curled up on the couch together watching TV. He calmed somewhat and flopped into her lap with a long, sad whine.

"Willow Bay beach," came the woman's voice, accompanied by the distinctive sound of fingernails clicking on a keyboard. "Suspected murder."

"Not suspected," Ali said firmly. "Definite murder." Her voice was coming out hypnotically, unemotionally. Not because she didn't feel anything but because of the effort it took to force herself to stay calm. She knew the woman on the line would flag this as suspicious, but it was better than Ali completely losing it and becoming hysterical.

The woman didn't react to her words. "Is the patient conscious?" she asked, speaking in a tone that told Ali she was reeling off a prompt from a screen.

"No...," Ali replied. "He's dead."

"Can you lean in and listen over his mouth to hear if he's breathing?"

"I already told you he's dead!"

"Can you see if his chest is rising and falling?"

"Listen to me," Ali snapped, finally losing her patience. "His skin is blue. He's dead."

There was a pregnant pause on the other end of the line. Then, "Ma'am? Do you know the victim?" Now, there was more than a hint of suspicion in her tone.

Ali tensed reactively. "Yes. I do. His name is Vincent Cole." As she spoke his name aloud, flashes of their interactions replayed in her mind. Their first meeting on the beach in the small hours of the morning. Their argument on the sand under the glaring eyes of the crowds. It was almost impossible to connect the man in her mind with this one lying dead and silent before her.

"And how do you know the victim, ma'am?" came the suspicious voice in her ear.

"He's an acquaintance."

"An ac-quain-tance..." The woman elongated the word, making it sound like a question.

Coming through the earpiece, Ali heard the distinctive sound of fingers rapidly typing on keys. She wondered what exactly the woman was writing down for it to be taking her so long. Sure, acquaintance was a big word, but it didn't have *that* many letters in it.

"Okay, I have cops en route to you now," the woman continued. "But I'm going to stay on the line with you until they get there. Can you tell me your name?"

"I'm Ali. Ali Sweet."

"Alright, Miss Sweet. They're two minutes out. Just hang on for me. And don't touch anything."

While it was reassuring to know that help was on the way and the huge burden of responsibility would soon be lifted from her shoulders, Ali also couldn't help but grow anxious. The first person to find a body was often the first suspect, and through the earpiece she could hear the woman typing again, her fingers rapidly hammering the keys.

'Now what is she writing?' Ali thought once more, and her pulse began to quicken with apprehension.

"Do you have any weapons on you, Ali?" came the intrusive voice in her ear.

"No."

"And are you on your own?"

"I'm with my dog."

"Is he on a leash?"

"No."

"Okay I'm going to need you to put him on a leash or remove him from the scene. The cops won't be able to approach if there's a dog on the loose."

Ali knew there was no point telling the woman Scruff wasn't dangerous, so she glanced around for something to tie him with. She spotted a piece of straggly blue rope lying in the sand, trash discarded by a fishing boat, she presumed.

She scooped it up and looped it around Scruff's neck, keeping the other tightly in her hand. He flashed her a perplexed look, and it occurred to Ali that he had never been leashed before.

"Sorry boy," she told him. Into the phone wedged between her ear and shoulder she announced, "Okay. He's leashed."

"Thanks. The cops are close. You should see lights any minute now."

As Ali sat there with Scruff, listening to the tapping keys in her ear mixing incongruously with the gently lapping waves behind her, her natural inner sleuth kicked into action, and she started to assess the scene in front of her for clues.

The first thing she knew with certainty was that Vincent Cole had been murdered. No one took their own life the day after coming into a handsome amount of money. With multiple stab wounds, no less. But who would want to kill the man? And why?

The fact he had just come into a very expensive rare antique seemed far too coincidental to Ali. The discovery then being broadcast on television, on a popular TV show, along with Vincent's name and face only added to her suspicions. Surely the most obvious motive here was theft? Although jealousy was also a viable option. But as she mulled the theories over in her mind, a new one came to her, and she felt her stomach drop with dread.

Revenge.

Revenge was a very common cause of murders. And who else had more reason to take revenge on Vincent Cole than *her? She* was the one who'd had a very public argument with Vincent Cole the day he'd died. *She* was the one he'd insulted. Vincent Cole's murder looked very bad for *her.* Any detective worth their weight would look at her first as the culprit!

51

A feeling of ice-cold dread swept through Ali, right from the crown of her head down to the tips of her toes. Despite the warm evening weather, she felt herself begin to shiver. The instinct to run overcame her. It was such a strong urge it took all her willpower not to succumb to it. But she held her ground because she knew it wouldn't be right. It wouldn't be fair to Vincent, who deserved justice. She had to stay and face the music, no matter how suspicious she looked and how much discomfort it might cause her. It would only be temporary, until the real murderer was caught, anyway, and that made her luckier than Vincent for sure.

Just then, she saw flashing lights coming from above her on the boardwalk along with the sound of thrumming car engines.

"They're here," she said to the woman on the phone.

"Okay, Ali. You can go ahead and hang up now. Good luck."

Ali thumbed the red button, ending the call, and was surprised to see a layer of cold sweat had transferred from her ear to the screen. She stood to flag down the cops, and wiped the sand from her behind.

But just as she was about to approach the boardwalk, her attention was diverted by the flashing lights of the cop car reflecting off the blade of the knife. Ali found her gaze falling once again to the murder weapon. In the bright lights, flashing through white, blue, and red, Ali noticed there was something drawn on the heavy wooden handle of the knife, something she'd not noticed before in the darkness. It looked like a crescent moon had been burned onto the surface.

'Pokerwork,' Ali thought, recalling the name of the technique since it was one that her talented friend Delaney was proficient in. She would use pokerwork to create bespoke signs for her customers using old driftwood she had found on the beach. Indeed, the sign for *Little Bits of This and That* was made using the very same technique.

Curious about the symbol, Ali wanted to take a closer look. But she didn't get the chance, because a face suddenly appeared on the boardwalk above her, freezing her in her tracks. It was the formidable Detective Elton.

"Miss Sweet," the detective said in her husky voice. "I hear you've stumbled upon a dead body. Again."

A horrible smirk twitched at the sides of her lips, and Ali felt her stomach drop to her toes. It sounded like Detective Elton was getting some kind of malevolent glee out of her being found in such a compromising situation and Ali cringed at just how distasteful that was. However much the detective hated her, a man was still dead at another's hands, and she ought to be more respectful.

"Where's Sebastian?" Ali asked, her gaze held steadily on the shiny surface of Detective Elton's sunglasses, where she could see only her own reflection.

"You mean *Detective Callihan?*" Detective Elton said, correcting her as she always did when Ali dared to refer to him by his first name. "That's none of your business."

Ali ground her teeth but said nothing more. Without Seb around to talk Detective Elton out of arresting her, it was better to stay silent and give her no ammunition.

So she watched silently as Detective Elton hopped over the side of the boardwalk and down onto the beach, the heels of her big, black leather biker boots sinking into the golden sand. She pushed her sunglasses up into her mass of dark wavy hair, and crouched down, clicking on her flashlight and shining into the space under the boardwalk.

Ali reflexively squeezed her eyes shut. She'd seen Vincent's dead body in the dimness, and it had been traumatizing enough; she didn't need to see him in the beam of a flashlight as well. But then she remembered the crescent moon she'd seen burned into the handle of the knife and forced herself to open her eyes.

In the beam of the flashlight there was no mistaking it now. The knife had a crescent moon burned into the handle. Whether that might be a clue as to the killer's identity or not, Ali wasn't sure, but she filed it away in the back of her mind.

"Well, well, well," Detective Elton said, standing up again, and clicking off her flashlight. "What a mess."

She beckoned for her forensics team, and they began swarming down from the boardwalk, flocking to the scene in their white coveralls and blue plastic booties, carrying their ominous black suitcases.

"You," Detective Elton said to Ali. She beckoned with a finger. "You're coming with me."

Ali swallowed the hard lump in her throat. "Where are we going?"

"Where do you think? I'm taking you down to the station. I think you and I need to have a conversation."

CHAPTER NINE

In the police station's interrogation room, Ali sat shivering, drumming her fingers impatiently on her knees. The air conditioning in the poorly lit room had been set to full blast, making goosebumps sprout along her exposed arms. The small room was filled with an irritating background buzz from the rusty looking aircon machine mounted in the corner, and the hard plastic chair she was sitting in was really starting to dig into her back. Ali couldn't help but assume the room had been deliberately set up in this manner to make anyone sitting inside feel extremely uncomfortable. And worse than all of it was that her trusty canine companion wasn't with her. Detective Elton had refused to let him in the police car and Ali had been forced to usher him away. The poor little guy had given her the most mournful expression she'd ever seen as he watched her drive away. When they next crossed paths, she'd make sure to give him the biggest, tastiest Jumbo bone as a way to apologize.

Ali peered impatiently at the clock on the wall. She'd been left alone in this bare room for an entire hour with nothing to occupy her mind but the same anxious thoughts looping over and over. Vincent's murder. The talk with her father. Vincent's murder. The talk with her father. Her troubled thoughts seemed to swing back and forth in her mind like a pendulum, and the *tick-tock-tick-tock* of the clock punctuating the *rattle-rattle-buzz* of the aircon seemed to vibrate around in her skull like water torture. She could feel a tension headache brewing.

The sound of the handle being pulled down brought Ali's attention back to the present moment. She turned in her chair as the door finally opened.

Her heart leapt instinctively with relief that her wait was finally over. But then it crashed right back down again when Detective Elton waltzed inside *without* Sebastian Callihan in tow. Instead, a burly uniformed cop followed in behind her. He had a shiny bald head like an egg.

"Where's Sebastian?" Ali asked, looking past the unfamiliar cop, craning to see if Sebastian was lurking in the corridor. She'd been in enough of these situations before to know the detectives always worked in pairs. Perhaps he'd been forbidden to come inside because of the "conflict of interest?"

Detective Elton's stilettoed boots clacked on the tiles as she walked behind Ali to her seat. "He's not coming."

A sudden *thud* made Ali jump in her seat and turn back round. Detective Elton had dumped a thick manila folder on the table in front of her. Ali knew this was just a technique to rattle her—Sebastian had told her as much. There was no way the detective already had a folder that thick on Vincent Cole; it had only been an hour since they'd been at the crime scene.

Detective Elton lowered herself into the chair opposite, sitting so awkwardly close to Ali their knees were almost touching. Uncomfortable with the proximity, Ali looked away. She made the mistake of stealing another quick glance at the door, something the hawkish Detective Elton immediately seized upon.

"I already told you," she barked. "He's not coming to save you."

Ali turned back to look at her. "Where is he?"

"Callihan?" She flashed a sinisterly triumphant grin. "He's been transferred."

Ali's heart skipped a beat. A wave of cold dread went through her. "Tra—transferred?" But they'd spoken just a few days earlier! He hadn't said a word to her about transferring! She couldn't believe the always thoughtful Sebastian would leave town without telling her.

"That's right," Detective Elton continued. "Officer Humphrey will be my second in command for our conversation." She pointed at the egg-headed man lurking silently in the corner and the words to "Humpty Dumpty" started involuntarily going round Ali's head.

"Why has Sebastian been transferred?" Ali asked. "And where to?"

Detective Elton sighed wearily. "Not that it's any of your business, but he's been assigned to a case out of town. A covert operation."

Ali's pulse spiked. A *covert operation*? That sounded ominous! "What exactly has he been transferred to do?"

"That's classified."

"Is it dangerous?" Images of shady black market criminal organizations were starting to flash through her mind. Sebastian wasn't like the stereotypical detective. He wasn't tall and muscular; he was sweet looking, boyishly handsome. He'd get eaten alive.

Detective Elton regarded her dispassionately. "All cop work involves an element of danger."

She was deliberately trying to rattle Ali. That much was obvious. But Ali simply couldn't stop it from working. Evidently, she cared more for Sebastian Callihan than she realized. "How long will he be gone for?"

"For however long the other force needs him," Detective Elton replied. "Days? Weeks? Months?" She gave a nonchalant shrug then fixed her dark eyes on Ali and stuck out her bottom lip into an exaggerated pout. "Why? Are you worried he'll miss your playdate? You two are dating now, aren't you?"

"Not to my knowledge," Ali replied, and she sat heavily back in her chair, her head swimming.

Yes, when she and Sebastian had seen each other a few days earlier, they'd talked about going on a date together. But no formal plans had been made. And now the thought of him being away for an undetermined amount of time made her feel suddenly very lonely.

She looked up at the detective. "Can you tell me what department he's been sent to at least?"

Detective Elton folded her arms and gave Ali a haughty look, her top lip curling into a sneer. "Why? So you know where to send your love notes?"

Ali's shoulders slumped. "Never mind," she murmured. This was useless. Detective Elton had always had a problem with her, ever since the first time Ali had wounded her pride by solving a case before her. But while Sebastian recognized that someone like Ali — naturally curious with a penchant for sleuthing and position in the community — could actually be a *useful* resource, Detective Elton had simply doubled-down on her dislike of her. Now, without her ally here, there would be no one to stop Detective Elton from hounding her. Possibly even arresting her.

"Are you done with your questions?" Detective Elton asked.

Ali nodded, glumly. "I'm done."

"Good." The detective tapped the manila folder on the table in front of Ali aggressively with her pointer finger. "Then let's talk about Vincent Cole. The victim. You told the operator he was an acquaintance. What exactly did you mean by that?"

"I just meant that I know who he is," Ali explained.

"How do you know him?"

"I don't. I met him once." She shook her head. "No, twice actually."

"Then tell me everything you remember about those two meetings." She sat back in her chair, folding her hands over her chest in a very relaxed posture.

Ali took a deep breath. There was no point lying, no matter how bad it made her look.

"The first time we met was on the beach the day before yesterday," she began, the moment replaying in her mind. "It was just before dawn, and I was at my bakery when I heard screaming coming from the beach. I thought someone might be hurt so I ran down to see. It was Vincent Cole. He'd just found a gold coin and was celebrating. That was the first time."

A small frown appeared between the detective's brows, as if she'd not expected Ali to be quite so forthcoming. "And the second time?" she prompted, waving an impatient hand.

"The second time was the next day," Ali continued, recounting the story carefully to make sure nothing could be misconstrued. "On the beach again. Only this time the reality TV show *Antiques Hunters* had turned up to film him. They put a porta potty up in front of my store for the crew, so I was speaking to one of the crew members, telling them to move it because they didn't have my permission to use the space. The crew member seemed to think that me complaining would make for interesting TV, but Vincent got irritated that the spotlight was on me and not him. He started insulting me and ... I lost my temper." She sighed and hung her head at the embarrassing memory. "We had a spat."

"A spat? Is that all?"

"Yes. We exchanged a few barbed comments back and forth. There were tons of witnesses, not to mention the whole thing was caught on camera."

"It was?"

This news had clearly piqued the Detective's interest. She sat up taller in her chair and peered at Ali with an eagerness in her eye.

"There'll be a clip online, I suspect," Ali continued. "It was all rather embarrassing. I said I'd throw his coin in the ocean and—"

Detective Elton again sat up in her chair, straight-backed and alert, and her dark brows shot up her forehead. Ali stopped speaking and watched the expression on the detective's face transform. Now she looked utterly thrilled. Over the moon. Ali got the distinct impression she'd given the detective some valuable ammunition.

"The gold coin is missing," Detective Elton announced triumphantly. "It wasn't on Vincent's person, and my team have been searching his hotel room for the last hour. It wasn't there either."

Ali was silent for a moment as she tried to make sense of why this was such a good piece of news to the detective. Then she put it all together. Vincent had probably been murdered for his coin. And *she* had just given herself a motive for wanting to take it. Not to sell or profit from it, but to throw it into the ocean out of revenge. No wonder the detective looked so gleeful. Even Ali thought she sounded guilty.

"I know what you're thinking," Ali said, her shoulders slumping.

"Oh? What am I thinking?"

But Ali stopped herself from saying more. She had to remember she was dealing with Detective Elton, not Detective Callihan, and anything she said would be twisted against her.

"I'd like to stop the interview here, please," Ali said.

"Are you sure?" the detective goaded. "Because if there's anything you've not told me, now is your chance to do it."

"I've told you everything I know," she replied. "And I'd like to leave. I'm not under arrest, am I? No? Then I don't have to talk to you."

"The door's there," Detective Elton replied, nonchalantly. "You're free to go."

Ali stood. But as she crossed the room for the exit, the detective spoke again.

"I'll be seeing you sooner or later, anyway."

Ali paused at the door. She understood a threat when she heard one.

"And make sure you don't meddle in this case," came Detective Elton's ominous warning from behind. "There's no Callihan to get you out of jail free this time."

Ali glanced back at her. The detective had turned fully around in her seat and had her fixed in the crosshairs of her laser-pointer glare.

"If I so much as get a whiff of you injecting yourself in this case, I *will* arrest you. Got it?"

Ali shoved down the door handle. "Loud and clear."

And with that, she marched out of the interrogation room.

*

It was dark by the time Ali made it home from the police station.

To her relief, Scruff was curled up asleep on the welcome mat outside her front door. His ears twitched at the sound of her approaching footsteps, and he raised his head, letting out a small bark of hello. The rope she'd looped around his neck on the beach was still there; Elton hadn't given her the chance to remove it before she'd been ushered into the back of the cop car.

"Hi Lil' Dude," she said, crouching down and gently unknotting the rope. She petted him apologetically between the ears. "I'm so sorry I left you behind. And I'm sorry I was gone for so long. You must be hungry."

He raised himself to all fours and barked.

Ali yawned and rummaged in her purse for her door keys. "I'm hungry, too. Detective Elton didn't even give me a sandwich. Can you believe it? Sebastian always makes sure I at least get a coffee..."

Scruff let out a low grumble to tell her just what he thought about Detective Elton's lack of manners, and Ali opened the door of her apartment. He bolted past her legs to get inside first, as he was wont to do, and in spite of all the worries swirling around in her mind, Ali couldn't help but chuckle at the cute habit.

He beelined right for the kitchen and barked.

"Hold up, I'm coming!" Ali called as she kicked off her sneakers and hit the light switch.

Despite the light, her small apartment looked even gloomier than normal. It was almost as if Vincent Cole's gruesome murder had vanquished all the light.

Ali paced over to the kitchen and fetched the kibble for Scruff. She also got out the promised Jumbo bone and unwrapped the shimmery red packaging for him. At the sound of that familiar crinkle, Scruff immediately brightened, and Ali knew all was forgiven.

As Scruff scarfed down his food, Ali yawned. "I don't know about you, but I'm exhausted. I don't even have the energy to make toast." Then she groaned with a sudden realization. "And the film crew are still in town, which means Piper will have her head in the clouds again tomorrow. You and I both know what that means. Burnt pastries." She petted his head as he munched. "I'm going to have to get up super early to get all the baking done." Then she remembered there was so much more to do tomorrow than simply bake goodies and run her store. There was a murder investigation going on, a murder investigation in which *she* was the prime suspect. And without Sebastian around she'd have no insight into what Detective Elton was doing. For the first time ever, she'd have no support in this case, and she'd have to clear her name all on her own.

"I'm going to bed," Ali announced, her stomach already beginning to churn with apprehension. "Don't stay up too long. We have work to do tomorrow, and I need my Doctor Watson for support."

Then she paced to her bedroom and flopped, exhausted into her bed. As she pulled the covers up to her chin, she reminded herself with determination that tomorrow she would solve Vincent Cole's murder and clear her name once and for all.

CHAPTER TEN

The shrill blaring of the alarm clock tugged Ali out of her slumber. She opened her bleary eyes, briefly disorientated by the abject darkness around her. Then she glanced at the clock. It was four AM. She groaned, remembering the reason she'd decided to set her alarm so early. She had to investigate Vincent's murder, clear her name, *and* bake all that morning's goodies.

Despite her fatigue, she forced herself up and out of bed. The quicker she got Detective Elton off her back the better. She knew the cops had a head-start because they always worked straight through the night on murder investigations. Sebastian had told her as much.

She quickly pushed the thoughts of Sebastian Callihan out of her mind before her concern about his absence derailed her. There would be time to worry about him *after* she had cleared her name.

She stumbled sleepily into the kitchen to feed Scruff and found him sleeping curled up beside his kibble bowl, an old habit she thought he'd progressed from. *Perhaps her Jumbo bone offering last night hadn't smoothed the waters between them after all*, she thought with a heavy chest.

Scruff looked up at her with big, brown, sleepy eyes as she padded toward him on bare feet.

"You look as tired as I feel," Ali said, pouring him a fresh bowl of kibble. "I hope I don't come back from my shower to find you asleep headfirst in your bowl."

Scruff let out a small bark in reply, and Ali headed off for her morning shower.

Inside the small bathroom, she turned on the shower faucet and stepped into the steaming jet. As the water sharpened her senses, Ali found her mind turning to Vincent and his murder.

'*Theft,*' she thought, recalling what Detective Elton had revealed back at the station. But was that the only motivation for the murder? Had the coin been stolen by the killer purely for its value, relegating Vincent Cole to nothing more than collateral damage in a crime of greed? Or was Vincent Cole targeted by one of the other treasure hunters because of jealousy? Revenge? At this stage, nothing was off the table, and Ali would have to thoroughly investigate any and every possibility.

She finished washing, then dressed and braided her wet hair. When she returned to the kitchen, she was pleased to see Scruff also seemed to have perked up. She collected all her belongings for the day and headed out of the apartment with her trusty canine companion in tow.

"Let's take the beach route," Ali told him as he trotted along beside her. "I want to see what's going on down there."

They walked the short distance to the beach, following the downward slope of the road to the sand. Despite the early hour, Ali was surprised to see plenty of treasure hunters there, their black silhouettes moving slowly across the sand with their metal detectors.

Had they been there all night, she wondered? Had anyone told them about the gruesome murder committed just a half mile along the beach from where they were scavenging? There was no way they hadn't noticed the police lights and all the commotion taking place near the pier, so perhaps they simply cared more about finding the treasure than they did about a man's life? Or, indeed, their own lives. Because there was a murderer on the loose, after all, and the only thing anyone knew for certain was that he'd killed Vincent and stolen the gold coin. How could any of them be certain they wouldn't meet a similar fate?

'Unless one of them is the killer...,' Ali thought, shuddering as she cast a wary eye across the treasure hunters.

Suddenly, being on the beach in the darkness seemed like a terrible idea. The treasure hunters had already shown her how rude they could be, and she didn't want to expose herself to undue risk.

Ali hastened her step, veering off the beach and onto the boardwalk where the glowing streetlamps and string lights gave her a sense of safety.

But when she reached the cozy boardwalk alcove shared with the two pizzerias, she was confronted by the terrible sight of the porta potties placed right in front of her door. With all the other stuff going on in her life, she'd completely forgotten about that particular annoyance.

She balled her hands into fists and looked down for Scruff, her confidant. Except Scruff was not standing beside her ankles as she expected.

"Scruff?" she said aloud, glancing around.

Then she spotted him trotting away along the boardwalk, disappearing in and out of the shadows between the beams of the streetlamps as he went. Her heart lurched as she watched him go. She'd really wanted his support today, but it seemed he still hadn't forgiven her for abandoning him yesterday evening.

Suddenly, something in her peripheral vision moved. Ali gasped and her heart jumped into her throat. She whirled around to see a figure moving out from behind the porta potty, a tall man in cargo pants and leather boots. It was...

"Dad?" she cried, pressing a hand to her thudding heart. "You scared the bejeezus out of me! What are you doing here?"

"You said we could hang out today while you worked," Richard replied simply. "Don't you remember?"

"Yes, I remember. But it's four-thirty in the morning!"

Richard looked confused. "Bakers start at dawn. That's right, isn't it?"

Ali's racing heartbeat began to slow. "Yes. That's right. But I wasn't expecting *you* to start at dawn."

Richard shrugged. "Oh well. In my day we all started at the same time."

Ali unlocked the door to the bakery. "In your day?" she asked as it yielded, and she stepped inside.

"From when I was a chef," Richard said, following after her.

Frowning, Ali turned to face him, her eyebrows raised with surprise. "You were a chef? When?" This was news to her.

"It's a bit of a convoluted story."

"Go ahead."

"Well, you know I was on a road trip in my RV?"

Ali nodded. She'd traced her father's years-long road trip along the old Route 66 using the postmarks on the letters he'd sent to her via her mother's home address on the way.

"Well, once I reached New York, I decided to keep going. I bought a boat ticket so me and my RV could cross the ocean together to Ireland and carry on the road trip from there."

Ali was astonished. None of his letters had come from overseas. "You went to Ireland? In a boat? How long did that take?"

"The crossing took about a week, but I ended up being on the boat for about three months in all."

Ali's eyes widened with astonishment. "Wait, wait, wait. Three months? Why? How? I can't even bear more than three hours in a plane, let alone three months on a boat."

Richard chuckled. "Actually, it was tremendous fun. I made friends with the chef. Hans. He was an eccentric German man. He taught me how to make all these strange European desserts. Before I knew it, I

was baking breakfasts with him most mornings. Unofficial sous chef."
He laughed at the memory. "I must've crossed back and forth across
that ocean ten times!"

He seemed amused by the nostalgic memory, but Ali found herself
stunned into the silence. The more she learned about her father's
wilderness years, the more of a mystery he seemed to her. What was
wrong with him that he'd prefer to work for free on a boat rather than
watch his children grow up?

She felt her shoulders begin to tense. "I'm surprised you didn't get
seasick."

Her father completely failed to pick on the tension. He raised his
eyebrows in evident amusement and proclaimed, "Oh, but I did!"

'Great,' Ali thought, bowing her head with dejection. So not only
had he chosen to be on a boat rather than be with her, but he'd even
preferred it when it had made him literally sick. And with that thought,
the memory of one of Lavinia Leigh's, the fortune teller, many
ominous warnings popped back into her head. *Do not trust the
wanderer.*

Ali quickly busied herself with opening the bakery's blinds, so her
father didn't see her pain. As she worked, he continued speaking.

"Good old Hans. He went back to Germany once the busy summer
season was over and I went back to New York, fired up the RV, and
decided to do Route 66 back to California again. Only it took me a lot
longer on the way back, because I spent more time at each stop on the
way."

'Years,' Ali thought, recalling the dates and postmarks of his letters
she'd plotted against a map.

Richard chuckled, "I wonder what Hans is up to these days?"

Ali almost blurted out that he clearly had a bad habit of falling out
of contact with people, but she managed to hold her tongue before it
slipped out.

"What did you learn to bake?" she asked instead. "Maybe I can get
you on croissant duty?"

"I can do croissants," he replied eagerly. "Danishes. Breads.
Whatever you need, really."

"Oh… great...," she'd only been joking— she was feeling overly
sensitive about one of the empty gaps in her father's life being filled by
his bizarre, trans-Atlantic baking expedition—but it was a bit late to
back out now. But at least with an extra pair of hands, the baking would
get done quicker, and she could focus her energy on the investigation.

As they went into the kitchen, Ali wondered if her father had heard about Vincent's murder yet. The inn where he was staying was nowhere near the scene of the crime, and he wouldn't have passed the pier or the police on his way here.

"So did you have a good evening in the end?" Richard asked in a suddenly stilted manner that reminded Ali she'd declined his invitation to go to dinner last night. And to think now, if she'd brave enough to go to the dinner and face her childhood fears she wouldn't have ended up in the middle of a murder investigation.

Her mind turning to Vincent's murder, she almost mentioned the dead body under the boardwalk but decided not to. Ignorance was bliss. Best to let her dad remain in the dark. Besides, she had no idea how he'd respond to the news. Would he comfort her or take a wide berth? She didn't want to risk finding out.

Once inside the kitchen, Richard poked his head into the fridge. "Very organized," he said. "Hans would approve."

"Of course," Ali replied, tensing her shoulders at the mention once again of the random German chef who'd spent a summer with her father instead of her.

He brought out the ingredients. "How much are we making, then?"

"I usually do batches of forty-eight," Ali said. "But it might be wise to do one or two less batches today since people might be put off coming in."

"Because of the porta potties?"

"Among other things."

Richard didn't seem to notice her comment. "You know, I was thinking about the porta potty dilemma last night."

"You were?" Ali was quietly touched her father had been thinking about her.

"Yes. I had an idea. You know the saying "If you can't beat them, join them?"

"Yes... but how does that apply to this situation?"

"Well, you currently have an empty store with a perfectly functioning bathroom, unused back rooms and a kitchen. Why don't you offer it up to the TV crew to use while they're here, on the condition they remove those dreadful porta potties?"

Ali considered it briefly. But her mind went to the horrible pinched-faced woman with the clipboard who'd taken such malevolent delight in her fight with Vincent. The last thing she wanted to do was help that cruel woman, even if she was only doing it to help herself. For all she knew, it was the clipboard woman who'd killed Vincent in the first place, just to get some footage for her show!

Ali halted. Could that actually be true? Detective Elton thought the motive for the murder was to steal the coin, but what if the coin was a ruse? A misdirection? What if the real killer was the clipboard woman?

Ali gasped and looked at her dad. "That's a great idea!" she said. The closer they were, the more she could look into them for clues.

Richard looked thrilled. "Oh. Good. Would you like me to speak to them once they arrive?"

"You'd do that?" Ali asked.

Ever since her dad had left, she'd been forced to grow up and take on all the responsibilities of the adult world. Teddy had stepped in as the parental figure to help guide her through life. But she'd never had her father actually offer a favor for her, and she had to admit it felt really good.

"Thanks. That would be really helpful."

Pleased to have a lead to pursue, Ali got to work baking with renewed vigor.

She was surprised by how incredibly smoothly the work went alongside her father. Where she and Piper often bumped into one another as they negotiated the small kitchen space, she and Richard seemed to move around more easily. Considering their conversation so far had been so awkward and uncomfortable, it was a surprise to find that cooking together came so naturally.

Then with a sudden heavy feeling, Ali realized why. They'd baked together when she was little, father and daughter sharing the activity. Indeed, that was the reason she'd started her bakery in the first place. And when it looked like her store was going to fail, it had been her father's famous coconut cupcake recipe that had saved her. She'd whipped up a batch, needing comfort, only for the cupcakes to become so popular they saved the bakery.

"All done," Richard said, putting the final batch in the oven.

"And early," Ali replied, her mind turning right back to the investigation.

They heard the bell go, and Piper appeared ready for her morning shift.

"Oh wow, you've already finished?" she asked in her sweet Southern accent.

"Yup," Ali replied. "With a bit of help." She smiled at her father, then removed her apron. "But I need to head out."

Richard's features twisted with confusion. "What? I thought we were going to spend some time together?"

"I know," Ali said. "But I have an errand to run. It's important. I need to get it done before opening."

"But Ali," Piper interrupted with a whine. "You said I could go to the beach for the filming!"

"And you can," Ali told her. "Later. Look, they're not even ready yet." She pointed out the window. There were a few *Antiques Hunters* crew members milling around with their headsets, clipboards and walkie-talkies, but they were clearly nowhere near ready for the day's filming. "So right now, I need you here manning the till and entertaining my father."

She threw the apron to Piper, who caught it with an exaggerated pout. Without wasting any more time, Ali left, exiting the bakery before either of them asked any more questions about her so-called errand. She didn't want to tell them about the investigation or being on Detective Elton's radar as a suspect. It would only worry them.

Out on the boardwalk, the sun was now shining. Ali maneuvered around the porta potties and looked out toward the beach to see it was now crawling with treasure hunters. It was time to start her investigation.

CHAPTER ELEVEN

Ali felt very conspicuous as she walked down the beach and into the thick sea of treasure hunters. Among the kooks and misfits, she was the odd one out.

It didn't take long for the whispers to start. Ali noticed people were going out of their way to avoid her, taking wide berths around her so they wouldn't have to cross paths. She wondered if it was because of her outburst yesterday during *Antiques Hunters*, or whether it was because the dreadful news about Vincent's murder had finally reached them, and someone knew she'd spent the evening being questioned at the station? There was only one way to find out. She'd have to bite the bullet and ask.

She turned to the closest detectorist, a man bent at the waist peering intently into the deep hole he'd dug in the sand, his features obscured by a messy mop of jet-black hair hanging greasily over his face.

"Excuse me," she said.

The man looked up, piercing her with angry, scowling eyes. "What?"

Ali's stomach dropped. She recognized the man. It was the same man who'd insulted Scruff yesterday morning. What bad luck that out of the hundreds of treasure hunters on the beach, she'd picked this one!

"Oh. It's you," the man said gruffly. "What do you want?" Then he looked around, a sneer curling his lip. "And where's that mutt of yours? He'd better not ruin my hole."

Ali rolled her eyes at the melodrama. "He's not with me," she said, feeling a pang of longing in her chest for her canine companion. Had Scruff been with her, he would probably have started growling at the rude man, picking up on the hostile negative energy oozing from him. But since he was off on his own adventure, just like Sebastian, Ali was going to have to figure this all out on her own.

She locked the man in her gaze. "I have a question to ask you."

He frowned at her. "Me?"

"Yes. You and the rest of the treasure hunters. I need some help."

"What makes you think anyone here will want to do you any favors? We all saw the way you blew up at poor Vincent." He shook his head disapprovingly, before adding, "And your dog is filthy." And

68

with that, he literally turned his back on her and went back to his precious hole.

Ali stood there, offended by the man's rudeness. *'He didn't even let me ask my question!'* she thought bitterly, folding her arms. She'd gleaned nothing from the frustrating conversation. Or had she? The man had called him "poor" Vincent. Perhaps that was an indication that he knew about his murder?

Ali put the frustrating exchange behind her and moved swiftly onto the next person.

"Excuse me," she said, tapping him on the shoulder.

The tall man turned around, his broad chest at Ali's eye-level, and she read the big bold letters across it. *Toronto Treasure Hunters.*

'You've got to be kidding me!' Ali thought. Wasn't there anyone on this beach she'd not had a run-in with?

"What do you want?" the man asked, brusquely, before his gaze darted around her face. "Wait. I know you. You're the bakery lady from yesterday, aren't you? The one who gave my coffee away to someone else!" His voice began to quiver with rage. "What do you want?"

Ali held both her hands up, palms facing out, as if in a truce. "Nothing," she muttered, shaking her head and backing away. If this guy was still holding a grudge about a thirty second delay caused by a black Americano mix-up, then he was already a lost cause as far as she was concerned.

Ali marched away, weaving her way through the bizarre people, searching for someone she hadn't already had a prior negative encounter with.

Just then, she spotted a group of people with dowsing rods and long robes. They looked like pagans or druids and she was absolutely certain none of them had been inside her bakery.

"Excuse me," she said as she marched toward them. "Can I speak to you about something?"

One of the men turned, his long brown beard stretching all the way to the middle of his chest like some kind of cartoon wizard. "You?" he said, eyeing her warily. "Aren't you the angry woman who threatened to throw Vincent's coin in the ocean? Why would I speak to a person with such volatile energy? Please go away. You're disrupting the vibration flows I am following."

Ali stopped in her tracks. This was utterly useless! She wasn't getting anywhere. None of the treasure hunters were going to speak to her because they all seemed to know what she was — the crazy bakery lady who had threatened one of their own. If she wanted to ask her questions, she was going to need to enlist some help.

She glanced back toward the boardwalk, her eyes falling to Delaney's craft store, *Little Bits of This and That*. She smiled to herself as a cunning plan began to form in her mind.

Then she marched off the beach for the boardwalk, knowing exactly what she needed to do to get these misfits to talk to her.

*

The boardwalk was drenched in sunshine as Ali marched past the new pet boutique en route for Delaney's store *Little Bits of This and That*. But suddenly she halted as something caught her attention.

She turned, looking at the inflatable dog bobbing in the breeze. Was that… Scruff? Ali couldn't believe it. It appeared Scruff and the inflatable dog were now friends!

'So that's where he went!' Ali realized, relieved to know his running off that morning hadn't been to snub *her*, but to check in with his new buddy.

She decided against interrupting him and continued on to *Little Bits of This and That*. It was only as she drew closer to the beautiful, gnarled wood door that she remembered the less than favorable way she had left Delaney the other day, with her lackluster response to the plans she had drawn up without her knowledge. Things had been left loose and unresolved, since Delaney wasn't at the store when she got back from her coffee with Teddy, and they'd not seen each other since. She hadn't had a chance to apologize properly for hurting her feelings. Would she still be mad?

Suddenly, the door to the store swung open and Delaney came rushing out. Her golden blond hair and sun-kissed skin glittered in the sunlight.

"Ali!" she cried. "I heard what happened last night. You must be exhausted."

She opened her arms wide for an embrace.

'Not mad, then,' Ali thought as she folded into them with a sigh of relief. Delaney's many bangles jingled in her ear as they hugged. "Are you okay?" she trilled.

"I'm okay," Ali said. "But I need your help."

Delaney moved back and held her by the shoulders at arm's length, peering at her intently with her sea-blue eyes. "That doesn't sound good."

"It's fine, I promise," Ali assured her. "It's nothing bad."

"Well you know I'd do anything to help you," Delaney implored, and she took her by the hand, guiding her inside the store.

Ali loved *Little Bits of This and That.* It was decorated as creatively as its owner with gnarled wooden shelves and a big round table with carved wooden stools painted to resemble toadstools. It always made her feel like she'd stepped inside a cozy log cabin in the middle of an enchanted forest rather than a store on the California coast.

"Do you want tea?" Delaney asked.

"Actually, no, I'm good. I just wondered if you could help me with a disguise."

Delaney was the thrift queen. She often brought old dresses, and even curtains, to reuse the fabrics in her handmade patchwork quilts. In fact, the gingham curtains in the bakery and the chintzy floral cushion had all been made by Delaney.

"A disguise?" she asked, blinking her long lashes. "Why?"

"I have a plan."

Delaney put her hands on her hips and gave her a stern look. "That's nice and vague."

"Sorry Delaney," Ali said. "I don't want you getting caught up in this. What you don't know can't hurt you."

"And by 'this,' you mean you're running your own investigation into Vincent's murder."

Ali blushed and looked sheepishly to her feet. "You know me so well."

Delaney harrumphed. "Fine," she said, reluctantly. "What do you need? Are we talking full-size Pikachu onesie or…"

"A disguise, Delaney. Not a costume. I just need to not look like myself."

"Okay, okay. I get it. Come with me."

They went behind the counter and through the door to the backroom, which was part Delaney's storeroom, and part art studio. It was chaos back there, full of tins of paint and boxes overflowing with materials.

Delaney crouched down beside a large leather case and opened it up. "I just found a whole load of 1970s housewife dresses at a charity store. Think Joni Mitchell in a wooden gypsy caravan going through the Scottish Highlands." She pulled out the first dress, a long-sleeve, floor-length dress in crimson and pink paisley swirls. "This is about the farthest from Ali Sweet as you can get."

That was true. Ali was a jeans, tee, and sneakers kind of girl. But she didn't think a '70s hippy folk singer dress would be enough to hide her true appearance. If anything, its peculiarity would only draw more attention to her.

"Do you have any sunglasses?" she asked. "A head scarf? Neckerchief?"

Delaney cast her a wary eye. "Are you trying to dress like a 1940s French spy?"

Ali rolled her eyes. "Delaney. Please! I just need people to not recognize me."

"Okay, okay!" Delaney went back to the trunk of clothes. She dug out a floppy straw hat, a red polka dot dress sundress, and a pair of fashionably oversized sunglasses. "How about this? If you let your hair loose as well, you'll look pretty different than usual."

"Good point," Ali said, pulling out her hair ties and weaving her fingers through her dark blond hair to shake out the braid. Since she always braided it straight out of the shower, it went super wavy when it was loose. That on its own was enough to make her appearance drastically different.

Ali quickly shirked off her clothes and slid into the sundress. She placed the sunhat on her head, pleased that the large brim covered her forehead and eyebrows, then slid on the sunglasses. She turned to face Delaney. "How do I look?"

"Different," her friend conceded, before biting down on her lip. "But Ali, I really wish you'd tell me what you're up to..."

"I know you would. But I'd really prefer not to. I don't want to drag you into this. Just remember I can handle myself. You don't have to worry."

Delaney rubbed her hands together anxiously, then finally relented with a nod. "Okay. I trust you."

"Thanks. And thanks for the costume." She was about to leave when she remembered about their disagreement from the day before. Things were evidently okay between them, since Delaney was being her usual overly helpful self, but Ali still felt it prudent to bring it up.

"You know, I'm sorry I wasn't more enthusiastic about your plans," she said. "They are really good. And I will definitely consider them; I'm just not confident in my ability to run a restaurant, that's all."

Delaney nodded. "Don't mention it, Ali. Seriously. It's in the past. Already all forgotten."

Ali gave her a grateful smile. Delaney really was the best friend a girl could hope for.

"Oh, wait! I have one more question to ask before I go."

"Oh?" Delaney asked, looking suddenly timid.

"Pokerwork," Ali said. "Has anyone commissioned you recently to do pokerwork for them?"

Delaney shook her head. "No. Why?"

Ali thought of the peculiar knife on the beach and the design burned into its heavy wooden handle. "I thought I might have found a clue on the beach. But I'm just clutching at straws really. It's probably nothing." She peered out the window toward the beach. "Well, I'd better go. Cross your fingers for me and wish me luck."

Delaney held up her crossed fingers, and with a final parting smile, Ali headed out, hoping that now she was going incognito, she might finally be able to get one of the treasure hunters to talk to her, and finally give her the lead she so desperately needed.

CHAPTER TWELVE

As Ali left *Little Bits of This and That* in her brand-new disguise, she passed Seth on his way in. At first, he didn't seem to notice her, his head bowed and his stride wide. It wasn't until Ali said his name that he even looked up.

"Seth?"

"Ali?" he said, visibly startling. "Hey. Wait, that *is* Ali, right? I can hardly recognize you. Did you change your hair?"

Ali smiled. That was certainly a good sign her costume was good enough! If Seth, whom she'd dated, had to ask whether it was her, then she was clearly on the right track!

"Yes, it's me," she told him, chuckling, before punctuating her sentence with an uncharacteristically girlish curtsy to fit with the uncharacteristically girlish dress.

Seth frowned in response, his thick dark brows drawing together with clear bemusement. "Why are you dressed like that?"

"Oh, just trying out a new look," Ali replied evasively, watching as Seth's gaze trailed all the way down to her toes peeping out from the pair of leather sandals Delaney had loaned her. He seemed taken aback to see her dressed in anything other than a pair of jeans, scuffed sneakers, and a *Seaside Sweets* shirt.

"It's a nice dress," he said, finally. "It suits you. It's very... Delaney."

Ali had to laugh. "Funny you say that. It *is* Delaney's. Dress, sandals, hat and all." It was a matter of fact now that the only times Ali ever got dressed up were because she'd either borrowed something from Delaney's closet or her friend had cajoled her into buying something she'd picked out during one of their shopping trips. She looked behind her at the carved wood door of her friend's store. "Are you on your way in to see her?"

Seth nodded, and there was a perceptible awkwardness to his movements. He lifted up a piece of driftwood from the beach that Ali had not noticed he'd been holding this whole time. "I'm bringing her this for an art project."

Ali paused and regarded him briefly. She couldn't put her finger on it, but something seemed off about Seth. His confusion at seeing her in

Delaney's dress seemed too pronounced, and his sudden awkwardness over the driftwood delivery seemed baffling, almost as if he'd been caught out. Ali wondered if it was the fact there had been yet another murder in their town that had unsettled him, especially since it had not been long since Seth himself had been a suspect in a murder investigation. Vincent's killing was probably bringing back some very bad memories for him.

"Is everything okay with you?" Ali asked her friend and former flame in a gentle voice.

"Of course," Seth said abruptly, so quick the question had barely left her lips.

Clearly, he didn't want to talk about it, and Ali couldn't blame him. If she could erase all the unfortunate murders that she'd witnessed she most definitely would. Deciding that Seth would bring up the murder if and when he needed to, Ali switched back to a conversational tone and flashed him a friendly smile. "Well, have fun with Delaney. I'll see you both later, I suppose."

"Yeah… okay… see you...," Seth murmured distractedly, and he didn't move as Ali turned on the spot and walked away.

It had been a decidedly weird encounter, but Ali put it out of her mind as she headed back toward the beach. Seth being in an odd mood was hardly the most important thing going on at the moment. She had a murder to investigate. And a persona to create.

She looked at the red polka dot fabric swishing around her as she marched, trying to think of an appropriate persona to fit with the disguise. She enjoyed playing roles, in no small part because of Teddy's long history of forcing her to be in whatever play he put on as a kid, although most of those roles were non-speaking and often inanimate. *"Just stand there and look like a tree,"* she heard Teddy's voice in her ear, and despite all the stress of the situation enfolding around her, Ali couldn't help but smile.

Just as she decided a tourist from the Midwest would be the perfect cover, she heard a bark from behind and turned to see Scruff standing by the pet shop. He was hanging out with his new inflatable friend.

Excited to see him, Ali decided to take a quick detour to say hello and hurried over. As she gained ground, she spotted Shauna the clerk with the long auburn hair through the window. The clerk appeared to be stomping angrily around an otherwise empty store, and Ali couldn't help but feel bad for her, even if she was as grouchy as Grinch on Christmas. She knew firsthand how daunting opening a business was after all, and how much courage it really took. For that blind leap of faith, to fail was a terrifying prospect. Perhaps, once all the *Antiques Hunters* fanfare had died down, she could try reaching out to her new neighbor again. Maybe even take Scruff in for the grooming session he apparently needed...

"Hi Lil' Dude," Ali said as she reached Scruff and his inflatable doggy friend.

She crouched to pet him and stretched her hand forward. But instead of nuzzling into her as he usually did, Scruff simply sniffed her hand warily, then barked at her like she was a stranger.

For a brief moment, Ali felt rejected. But then she remembered she was wearing a disguise and realized that Scruff had simply failed to recognize her.

She laughed and straightened up. That was two for two now. If a man she'd dated and a dog she pretty much owned didn't recognize her, then her outfit was surely good enough to fool at least *one* of the treasure hunters into talking to her!

Emboldened, Ali headed back to the beach to try her luck a second time.

When she reached the beach, her feet sank into the golden sand. Delaney had lent her sandals for the disguise and the sensation of warm sand between her toes was rather pleasant. She didn't get much time to enjoy the beach since she was always so busy with the bakery, but now was not the time and so she raced on.

She beelined straight for the closest woman she didn't recognize, a portly woman in a bright purple t-shirt with puffy, dyed black hair. She looked pretty normal. For a detectorist, at least.

"Excuse me," Ali said, putting on her best, affable Midwest accent. "May I ask you a question?"

The woman stopped what she was doing and smiled — actually *smiled!* A wave of relief washed through Ali. It was the first time any of the treasure hunters had been anything other than rude to her.

"Sure," the woman said, turning off her buzzing metal detector and leaning on it like a staff. She was wearing thick black framed glasses that were slipping down the bridge of her red, shiny nose from the heat. By the almost translucent white color of her skin, it was obvious she wasn't from these parts and was suffering in the California sunshine.

Ali lowered her voice conspiratorially and leaned in. "I heard this rumor going around," she said with a twang of innocence. "I was wondering if you might have heard it too?"

"Is it about Vincent Cole?" the woman whispered back.

Ali nodded. "It is. About his coin. Did you hear?"

"That someone killed him and stole it?" the woman replied, matching Ali's conspiratorial tone. "Yeah, I heard. We all heard. Tragic, isn't it?"

Ali's heart began to race. Finally, she was getting somewhere!

She nodded. "So tragic. I don't suppose you have any idea who killed him?"

"Actually, I do," the woman said, wiggling her brows excitedly, before announcing, "It was the woman who owns the bakery."

Ali's heart sank, her hopes dashed. The grinning woman leaned proudly and triumphantly on her staff as she continued relaying the rumor Ali already knew. "I've never met her myself but everyone's saying she's a lunatic. A serial killer. Apparently, she commits crimes with her lover who's a detective. That's how she gets away with it."

"Gee…," Ali said, fighting to keep up her persona as her mind turned over the preposterous accusations once again. "She sounds like a real mean piece of work."

Just then, the man working beside the purple-shirted woman craned his head to look at them. He was a long-haired hippy type, bare-chested, with a slim torso and several big-beaded necklaces dangling around his neck. Ali instantly got cult-member vibes from him.

"Sorry to interrupt," he said in a slow, day-dreaming voice. "But I overheard you guys talking about Vincent Cole."

The purple-shirted woman looked at him eagerly, and Ali felt a second spark of hope light inside of her. Perhaps *this* was the breakthrough she was hoping for.

"What about him?" she prompted.

The hippy man scratched his bare chest. "I heard he was murdered by a devil worshipper."

Ali's eyebrows flew up. Meanwhile, the purple-shirted woman standing beside her nodded like this was the most obvious development.

"I heard that too!" she agreed. "The bakery lady. She's into witchcraft."

The hippy man nodded, and his hand went instinctively to one of the beaded necklaces hanging round his neck, taking hold of the pendant hanging off it that Ali now saw was a large crucifix.

"You guys need to be careful," he warned. "Rumor is she curses people and makes voodoo dolls out of pastry to torture them."

The purple shirted woman shuddered. "Thanks for the heads up."

Now Ali really had to bite her tongue. What was wrong with this crazy bunch of conspiracy theorists? She'd never heard anything so ridiculous in all her life, yet they were eating it up without even the smallest scrap of proof. But then again, they all seemed to be a few sandwiches short of a picnic.

Ali decided that speaking to the treasure hunter crowd wasn't going to get her anywhere. If the general consensus was that the murderer was a magically imbued pastry-witch enacting random baking-related curses on innocent strangers, then she needed to treat every single thing that came out of their mouths with a grain of salt.

Tuning out the gossiping of the hippy man and purple-shirted woman, Ali put her hands on her hips and glanced around at the people on the beach. Any one of them was more likely to be the actual murderer than she was! But suspecting one of their own was harder than believing a strange rumor.

Suddenly, Ali was struck by a new thought. If all the detectorists had heard the same rumor, then it stood to reason that it had originated from within their group. They kept themselves to themselves, after all, barely interacting with any of the locals. So one of them had to have been the one to start the rumors in the first place. And why? To throw the eye of suspicion away from themself! Because *they* were the killer!

Which meant if she could trace the rumors back to the source, she may well find the killer that way.

Her heart began to beat with rapid excitement, and she turned back to the pair. "Hey, so where did you guys hear about this demon baker lady from?" she asked, almost forgetting her Midwest accent in her excitement.

The hippy glanced about himself, looking for someone, then finally pointed into the distance. "I heard it first from that guy."

Ali followed his finger, squinting against the glare of the sun, until her gaze found a very old man sitting on his backside, sifting slowly through the sand with a pan. "Him?"

The hippy nodded. "Yeah."

"I did too," the purple-shirted woman added. "He's been in the treasure hunting game for a really long time. He knows everybody. He's very trustworthy."

Ali regarded the frail old man. There was absolutely no way someone *that* old could stab a healthy middle-aged man like Vincent to death. He couldn't even stand up in the sun to search for treasure. He was literally having to sit down to search for metal, panning the sand like someone from a bygone era panning for gold.

Her hopes were dashed once again. The man *wasn't* her killer, she was absolutely sure of it. But he *was* the person who'd started the rumors about her, and that in itself was a curiosity worthy of pursuit.

She turned to the gossipy detectorists, who were still sharing rumors about her. "Good luck with your searches." Then she turned and walked away in the direction of the old man, far from convinced anything would come of this new lead.

When she reached him, she plonked herself down beside him on the sand.

"Lovely weather here, isn't it?" she said in her lilting Midwestern accent.

The old man looked at her and squinted. "What?"

"I said it's lovely weather," Ali repeated.

The old man sneered, "It's too hot."

Ali smiled affably. "I suppose it is."

Silence fell. The old man clearly wasn't in a sociable mood. But if what she'd heard about him from the others was true, she knew he could be loose-lipped given the right circumstances...

"I have a question about Vincent Cole," she said, jumping straight to the chase.

"The guy who got killed?" the old man said, his expression brightening immediately. "What do you want to know?"

"I just found out how he died. It was voodoo. Cursed pastry. Apparently, the bakery owner is a witch. Did you hear anything about this?"

The old man pressed his thin lips into a tight line. "Maybe."

"Maybe?" Ali pressed. "People around here say you're the one they heard it from first. I thought maybe you'd seen something, or had a run-in with the witch or something—"

Ali trailed to silence as she realized the old man's shoulders had started to shake. She regarded him curiously, wondering what was going on. Then she worked it out. He was laughing! Something she said had provoked this sudden outburst of laughter.

He held his hands up in truce position. "Ah, you got me," he said through his chuckles. "Guilty as charged."

Ali's frown deepened as she grew more perplexed. "I'm sorry? I don't understand."

The man's chortles died out. "I made it all up! The witch. The cursed pastry." He tapped his head with a wizened old finger. "I invented the whole thing."

Ali couldn't help herself. She pouted. This old man had been spreading rumors about her for *fun*? With no regard for the very real human being whose reputation was being tarnished in the process? What a cruel way to get his kicks!

But of course, she was in disguise, and didn't want to reveal her true identity. She forced her face into a blank mask. "Why did you make up the rumors?"

"Because this lot are a bunch of odd balls! They believe anything I tell them. They seem to think I'm some kind of oracle." He guffawed again, before adding, "When you get to my age, you get your kicks where you can."

Ali's chest deflated. So the man had simply spread the rumors for fun to tease the gullible conspiracy theorists among the group, and he'd dragged *her* name through the mud in the process.

"A man is dead," she reminded him. "That's nothing to joke about. People are on edge, and for good reason. Why add more confusion and fear to an already troubling situation?"

The old man let out a weary sigh, "I don't know. Everything has changed since my day. I'm sick and tired of it. Look at what these young 'uns are doing to the beautiful beach. No respect anymore. With their buzzing machines, making potholes all over the place like a bunch of gophers." He tutted and shook his head. "And don't get me started on the TV show!"

Ali glanced across the beach to see the *Antiques Hunters'* crew had finally mobilized for the day. Mullet Man and his orange microphone seemed particularly focused on a group of ditzy-looking, bikini-wearing women who Ali suspected had no clue what they were actually supposed to be digging for. She rolled her eyes, feeling an affinity with the old man, and turned back to face him.

"I'm not a big fan of the TV either," she told him. "Shows like that exploit people. Mess with their emotions. Goad them until they snap." She thought back bitterly to the argument she'd had with Vincent that had been provoked for the sake of TV drama. Thanks to the TV crew, she had ended up right in the middle of this horrible mess of a murder investigation.

"It's not just them," the old man continued. "Ferdinand is the worst."

"Ferdinand?" Ali asked. "Who is that?"

The man shuddered. "He's the most awful man you'll ever meet. A creep. A jerk. He goes all over trying to find treasure, filming it for his show."

He sneered with distaste, and Ali turned the new information rapidly over in her mind. There was *another* antiques show? *Antiques Hunters* wasn't the only in town filming the treasure hunt? She needed to know more. This may well be the lead to crack the case wide open.

"Who is he?" she pressed. "What is his show? What channel is it on?"

The man shrugged. "I don't know what his show is called. It's on the *internet*." He spat out the last word and scoffed in evident disapproval of the internet's existence. "He calls himself an *influencer*." He spat the second word out even more disgustedly, and now redness was starting to creep up his neck. "As if that's a proper job! In my day, we worked real jobs! In factories! Now the kids just flounce around on YouTube and call it a hard day's work!" He bashed his hands onto the sand on either side of him. "Pah!"

Ali inched back. She wasn't sure what to make of the man's angry tirade. Was Ferdinand *actually* a jerk or did the old man just dislike the way the treasure hunting world was modernizing? He preferred to use a pan over a metal detector, was furious about the very existence of the internet, and despised the new generation of treasure hunters so much he teased them with outlandish rumors. She didn't put much stock in his words. But the mysterious Ferdinand and his internet show had piqued her curiosity, and she knew she wouldn't be able to rest until she'd checked him out for herself.

"Which one is Ferdinand?" she asked the old man as she gazed out at the crowds of detectorists.

The old man looked at her like she was crazy. "He's not here!"

"He's not?" Ali asked, confused. "But I thought you said he was making a treasure hunting show."

"He is, he is!" the old man snapped impatiently. "Just not here. He's somewhere else."

"Oh."

"He's in competition with *Antiques Hunters*. They hate each other. He always tries to beat them to the treasure."

Ali's chest fell. If Ferdinand wasn't even in Willow Bay, then he wasn't a good candidate for theft and murder! Her lead had gone cold before she'd even had a chance to look into it.

But then a new thought hit her, and she did an about-face. According to the old man, Ferdinand was trying to make a rival version of *Antiques Hunters*. Out of the three motives she'd been considering for Vincent's murder, jealousy and rivalry were two of them. She didn't know how yet, but perhaps the "creepy" Ferdinand had something to do with Vincent's killing after all?

Ali's heart thudded with anticipation. She looked at the old man. "Do you know where Ferdinand is at the moment?" she asked.

He shook his head. "It will be on the internet, won't it?"

"Yes! Of course! Thank you!"

Ali leaped up, leaving the cantankerous old man behind her as she paced away and got her cell phone from her pocket. She went onto YouTube and typed *Ferdinand* into the search bar, along with the word *treasure*.

His channel immediately appeared on her screen.

Ali clicked on the most recent video, noting the date showed it had been released on the site less than twenty-four hours earlier.

As the video began to play, showing a lush green grassy field and several close-up shots of muddy, artistically placed digging tools, Ali was surprised by the slick production value. Unlike *Antique Hunters,* with its goofy Eddie Expert character and Mullet Man waving his oversized orange microphone, Ferdinand had chosen an altogether more somber and serious tone for his channel. The editing was like something from a car advertisement, with cool electronic beats playing in the background over artistically shot scenes.

"Hi guys," the man on the screen Ali presumed was Ferdinand said. "I'm here at the battlefield in Wave Bay…"

"Wave Bay!" Ali exclaimed with sudden surprise.

That was just up the coast, a short drive from Willow Bay! Ferdinand could easily have traveled to Willow Bay from Wave Bay in order to murder Vincent.

Her hands began to shake with excitement as she looked back down at the screen. From the way Ferdinand presented himself on screen, Ali got a very bad vibe frin him. He was coming across as a self-important tool, and she could certainly feel a creepiness in his demeanor. But did that make him a murderer?

There was only one way to find out. Ali would have to go to the battlefield in Wave Bay and question Ferdinand herself.

CHAPTER THIRTEEN

Ali hurried to the parking lot around the back of her apartment block where her car was parked. She drove along the coastal road in the direction of Wave Bay. She had been to the town once before while following a lead for her father. When the lead had turned out to be incorrect, she'd been devastated. But now her father was back in her life...and she'd been forced to leave him to investigate a murder!

Suddenly, Ali realized her "errand" was taking her far longer than she'd intended. She'd left Piper the perpetual klutz to man the bakery all on her own, and her chronically restless father sitting around with nothing to do. As soon as she found the battleground, she'd give them a call to make sure the bakery wasn't burning to the ground.

Just then, she spotted the welcome sign for Wave Bay.

"Remember this, Scruff?" she said, turning toward the passenger seat where her trusty companion usually sat. But of course, Scruff was not there, and her chest sank with disappointment. Her canine companion had been by her side since her very first investigation but now he had chosen his new inflatable friend over her. Though to be fair to him, she had been wearing a disguise that had fooled him into thinking she was someone else. Either way, she was doing this alone without support from her favorite furry fellow.

She reached a T-intersection and slowed to a stop, peering out the windshield as she tried to work out which way to go. Since she was already somewhat familiar with Wave Bay, she made an educated guess as to which direction the battleground from Ferdinand's YouTube video was; and she turned left, away from the ocean and toward the rolling green fields.

Her guess was quickly proven correct. She was soon passing signs for a historic battlefield.

Before long she reached a muddy parking lot. It was surprisingly full, with dozens of cars packed in side-by-side. Among them was a very expensive looking Mercedes.

"Bingo!" Ali cried. It was exactly the sort of car she expected a self-important man who made slickly produced YouTube videos to drive. This had to be the place.

She parked her car and killed the engine. She was about to jump out and start her investigation when she remembered her vow to make sure everything was okay at the bakery. She grabbed her cell instead and dialed the store line.

Piper answered after the first ring. "Seaside Sweets," she said in her sweet Southern accent. "How can I help you?"

"Pipes, it's me."

"Ali! Hey! Where are you? You've been gone ages! *Antiques Hunters* have been filming for like an hour now and I'm missing it." There was a whiny quality to her voice that rubbed Ali the wrong way. She'd prefer to be at the bakery given the choice, and it irked her that Piper was getting to spend all this time with her father while she was otherwise engaged.

"I'm sorry," she told her assistant. "But my errand is taking way longer than I expected."

"Well, I'm not surprised since you've driven all the way to Wave Bay."

Ali's eyes widened with astonishment. How did Piper know where she was? Had she been getting mind-reading lessons from Lavinia Leigh?

"How do you know I'm in Wave Bay?" she asked.

"I'm following you on the Track My Friends app. When you took longer than we were expecting, Richard started to get worried, so I showed him how the app works and how it can track people. It showed that you were in Wave Bay. We thought you might have been abducted but then I remembered that fancy organic store you love is in Wave Bay and figured you'd gone there. Did you know Richard's *never* owned a smartphone?"

Ali paused, needing a moment to assimilate Piper's monologue. Her assistant had a frustrating habit of talking super quickly while flitting between many different topics. Sometimes Ali didn't even know which bit to reply to first.

"When did you put a tracking app on my phone?" she asked.

"Back when I was going on all those dates, remember? You were worried I was going to meet a psycho, so we downloaded the app."

Ali sighed. She remembered. She just hadn't realized it would give Piper the ability to track *her* in return. She really was woeful with technology. Clearly that was another thing she and her father had in common.

"Well, it's nice to hear you two are getting along so well…," Ali murmured, feeling slightly aggrieved that Piper was getting to know things about her father before she did.

"Oh yeah. We clicked right away," Piper replied, failing to pick up on her tone.

"Best buddies!" came the muffled voice of Richard from the background.

Ali found her hand tightening around the phone. She should be pleased her dad was fitting into her new life so seamlessly, but it rankled her for some reason.

"So?" Piper's voice said in her ear.

"So what?"

"So why are you in Wave Bay?"

Ali hesitated. What kind of errand would take her all the way to the next town along the coast? She racked her brains, then realized Piper had already provided her with the cover story.

"Almond essence," she said. "That organic store in Wave Bay is the only place that stocks the 100% non-additive version I use in the macarons."

Though Ali couldn't see her, she could practically hear Piper rolling her eyes. Her assistant didn't understand why she insisted on using such expensive ingredients, but her pallet wasn't as refined as Ali's was, and she hadn't spent a year studying under Milo Baptiste, the famous French pastry chef, having him drum it into her. And while her point that none of the tourists in Willow Bay had refined pallets either held true, Ali just couldn't help herself.

"She's buying almond essence," she heard Piper repeat, clearly for Richard's benefit.

Just then, Ali spotted a car turn into the lot behind her, bumping along the uneven earth as its tires squelched through the mud. Ali watched as the engine cut out and a young woman emerged from the driver's side with her eyes glued to a cell phone. She peered up at the sign for the battlefield, then back down at her phone, then took off across the field. She was clearly looking for something, using a map on her phone or her GPS, and Ali wondered whether she was also looking for Ferdinand. She decided to follow her.

"Piper, I have to go," she said, opening her door and hopping out the car.

"Please hurry back," Piper exclaimed. "I don't want to miss my big opportunity."

"I'll be as fast as I can," Ali assured her. She locked her car behind her. "But can you do me a huge favor?"

Piper sighed loudly. "Yes. What is it, boss?"

"Can you keep my dad away from anything murder related? I don't want to scare him away."

"I can try," Piper said.

"Thanks," Ali said.

She ended the call and slid her phone back into her pocket, then took off across the field behind the woman.

As she marched on, she regretted not having changed out of Delaney's costume before coming here. The mud was squelchy, and she found herself slipping and sliding in her attempt to keep up with the fast-walking woman. She squinted ahead as she marched, looking for any sign of the "creepy" Ferdinand, until she finally spotted a crowd of people with metal detectors. The woman she'd been following sped up, surging away in that direction with an excited spring in her step.

"That's got to be him," Ali said, hastening to keep up.

As she drew closer, she scanned the scene until she found Ferdinand. He was standing under an awning some distance away from the people with metal detectors, his arms folded in a self-important posture that reminded Ali of a movie director. The combination of a trilby and a snood he was wearing added to the effect.

Ferdinand was talking to a group of people who, even from this distance, Ali could see were fawning all over him. When the woman she'd been following rushed up to the crowd, Ali realized what was happening. Creepy Ferdinand had *fans*.

She paused, trying to make sense of what she was seeing. It appeared that Ferdinand had an entire team of people working around him, and it suddenly occurred to Ali that he didn't actually do any of the treasure hunting himself. Nor the digging or scanning. He employed people to do the dirty work. He was merely the face of the operation. Less *treasure*-hunter and more *adoration*-hunter. Ali wondered if he even actually cared about treasure at all, or if he'd just found a niche to exploit for YouTube views.

Curious, she continued onwards until she got close enough to hear what he was saying that was so riveting he had a group of people hanging off his every word.

"So you guys know from last week's video that I've been digging in the Scottish Highlands," he said in a lazily arrogant voice. "And I found that whole load of silver swords. Well, it's like ninety-nine percent certain that they belonged to some ancient dead king. They're being valued at the moment and it's looking like they'll come to over a million dollars." He said it nonchalantly, like this was no big deal. Chump change to add to his stacks of riches. "I'm in discussions with the Scottish government now to secure a price to buy them back. They're furious I took them out of the country. But that's life. Finders-keepers, right?" He guffawed, and his fans laughed along with him. "So, who wants an autograph?"

As his fans began shoving things at him to sign, Ali's toes curled with secondhand embarrassment. Ferdinand's story about his trip to the Scottish Highlands had really shone a light on the type of person he was: someone who didn't have any qualms about behaving unethically to get what he wanted in life. And someone who didn't actually need any more money but was going to go to extreme lengths to get more of it anyway.

Maybe he'd coveted Vincent's gold coin? Maybe he'd sent one of his workers to do his dirty work on his behalf? Maybe he'd gotten a fan to do it? The possibilities were endless, and Ali knew she would have to turn her Midwestern charm all the way to the top if she stood a chance of getting him to talk.

Mentally preparing herself with her fake persona, she drew up to the edge of the crowd and began to worm her way through them.

"Ferdinand!" she cried, channeling Piper. "Ferdinand! My name's Ali and I'm your biggest fan!"

He looked up from the paper he was signing and grinned at her. "Hi Ali. I don't think I've met you before. Do you want me to sign something?"

"I don't have anything," she said. "I just wanted to talk to you. I really like treasurer hunting and I wondered if you heard about the hunt happening in Willow Ba—"

He cut her off mid-sentence with a question of his own. "Do you want to be in the video?" he asked, abruptly, pointing over to a camera man busy filming the excavation work.

His question drew a jealous gasp from the audience. The woman closest to Ali shot her a daggered look.

Ali blushed. "Gee, no. I'm too shy to be on film," she bluffed.

"Why?" Ferdinand replied. "A pretty girl like you shouldn't be shy."

Ali cringed all the way to her toes and squirmed under the jealous glares of the other girls around her. She blamed Delaney's dress. If she'd turned up in her usual batter-splattered jeans "famous Ferdinand" would not have looked at her twice.

Mustering all her willpower, Ali managed to fake flattery. "Thanks, that's sweet," she said, twirling a chunk of thick blonde hair in her fingers. "But I'm only here to see the dig. I've been at the one in Willow Bay. Have you heard about it?"

Ferdinand instantly sneered. "Willow Bay. Yeah. It's full of quacks who think there's Viking gold in the sand or something stupid. Don't they know the Vikings landed in Canada? Which reminds me of that Viking drinking goblet I found in Newfoundland."

He launched into another heroic story and his fans stared at him with adoration.

"—It's Spanish gold," Ali corrected, raising her voice to be heard. "Not Viking treasure."

Ferdinand halted and looked at her with a frown. He clearly wasn't used to being interrupted. "Excuse me?"

"I said they're searching for Spanish gold," Ali re-iterated. "Not Viking treasure. And what makes you so certain there's nothing there? The *Antiques Hunters* show is filming there, so they obviously think it's something."

Just then, one of the metal detectorists working nearby turned to look at her, his weary look of underappreciation giving Ali the impression he'd prefer to be on the beach of Willow Bay himself searching for gold rather than out here at the battlefield. He stopped what he was doing and looked at Ferdinand. "Didn't I say we should go to Willow Bay?"

The change in Ferdinand was instant. His features suddenly twisted into an angry scowl, and he marched up to the man. "Shut up, Greg," he spat. "When are you going to get it through your thick head that I'm not paying you to have opinions. If you want to forgo your next check to go dig up a beach like a peasant then be my guest, but you won't find anything."

Ali was shocked by his rude outburst. But more shocking was Greg's complete lack of reaction. He was clearly used to being treated like this by his boss, which made the whole unpleasant scene altogether worse.

Ferdinand, though, was not done. He turned to the rest of the demoralized looking detectorists around the site and threw his arms out. "Does anyone else want to go to Willow Bay to look for fictitious gold? Or are you going to accept that I have a sixth sense for this kind of thing. That there's a reason why *I'm* the most successful treasure hunter in the world and you're all just the useless schmucks who work for me!"

The team of diggers and detectorists lowered their eyes, evading eye contact in a way that seemed almost routine to Ali.

"Thought so," Ferdinand snapped, and with that he stormed away to a nearby trailer, slamming the door behind him.

To Ali's surprise, his group of fans went flocking after him like a bunch of ducklings following their mother. Clearly his rude, angry tirade had done nothing to dampen their affection towards him. How *anyone* could support that kind of behavior baffled Ali.

She kept her face as still as she could, but inside she was stunned and fighting the natural instinct to raise her eyebrows as high as they could possibly go. The old man on the beach was right. Ferdinand was a creep and a total jerk. He'd gotten so riled about the Willow Bay situation he'd taken it personally and unleashed his rage on a bunch of innocents.

Ali thought back to her conversation with the old man on the beach. He'd told her Ferdinand was trying to start a rival antiques show. Maybe that was why he was so annoyed? Because the *Antiques Hunters* show was more popular than his? And because they'd actually found treasure when his so-called "sixth sense" had failed to turn up anything of any worth?

But more than just that, if he could show his temper that quickly with just the smallest of provocations, could he have killed Victor in a rage to get hold of his treasure? There was only one way to find out. She needed to know if he'd been in Willow Bay the night of the murder. And she knew just the person to ask.

She approached Greg. After Ferdinand had blown up in his face, he'd gone back to his work, and was glumly digging in the dirt.

"Are you okay?" Ali asked him.

He looked up at her and shrugged his shoulders. "I guess. He's always like that. Nothing I can't handle."

"I hope he pays you well."

Greg let out a wry laugh. "Let's just say I get my bills paid on time and leave it at that."

Ali grimaced. She felt bad for him, and Piper by extension, since she'd reneged on her promise to let her follow the film crew around. Once she got back to Willow Bay, Ali vowed to be nicer to her assistant and show her appreciation more often. But first, she needed to dig further into the character and movements of the explosive Ferdinand.

She turned her focus back to Greg. "Can I ask you a question?"

Greg's brows twitched with bemusement. He evidently wasn't used to people wanting to talk to him. He was probably so downtrodden by his overbearing boss it didn't even cross his mind anymore that someone might want to speak with him.

"Me?" he said with a curious inflection. "I mean, I guess..."

Ali smiled in an attempt to put the suspicious man at ease. "Do you know if Ferdinand went to Willow Bay at any point yesterday?"

Greg regarded her for a moment longer, then sighed visibly, and dropped his eyes back down to his hole. It didn't take a huge leap for Ali to guess the reason for his change in demeanor. He'd thought she was going to speak to him only for that brief moment to be dashed the second she brought up Ferdinand. As regrettable as Ali felt to have added to his demoralization, she had no choice but to carry on and get the information she needed.

"No," Greg said, directing his voice into the hole as he jabbed it aggressively with his spade.

"Are you sure?"

"One hundred percent. We reached the battleground at seven AM. Set up the equipment. Had a coffee and strategy meeting. Then we started live streaming the dig at about midday." He didn't look at her as he spoke, instead digging the hole with the sort of grumpy ferocity Ali would expect from a child.

"How long were you streaming for?" she asked, trying to sound as personable as she could considering she'd clearly upset Greg even more than he already was.

"Ten hours," he replied brusquely. "At least."

"Ten hours?" Ali echoed with surprise, her eyebrows shooting all the way up. "You were digging for ten hours straight?"

She really couldn't believe it. Who in the world would choose to spend *ten hours* of their precious time watching people *dig holes*?

Greg leaned on the handle of his spade and looked at her with narrowed his eyes. "I thought you said you were a fan…"

Ali quickly realized her mistake. A true fan would already know how long Ferdinand streamed for. "Oh. I am. I'm just annoyed that I missed the stream because I was driving all of yesterday to get here."

"Well, you didn't miss much," Greg replied, seemingly buying her excuse. "We didn't find anything, and Ferdinand was furious. No one likes a fruitless stream. Not us, not the viewers, and definitely not Ferdinand." He sighed, "It messes up our YouTube stats too."

Ali pondered what he was saying. There were so many more important things in life than YouTube stats, but that wasn't the issue.

The important thing was that Ferdinand *hadn't* been in Willow Bay at the time of Vincent's killing, and he also had video evidence as an alibi to prove it. Which meant her lead had gone cold.

Greg turned back to his hole. "At least if we'd gone to Willow Bay we could have streamed about the murder. That's way more exciting than a bunch of people failing to find anything in a battleground. But Ferdinand said the town is really weird and none of the local stores want the treasure hunters there."

"Oh?" Ali asked, surprised. Beyond her own complaints about the film crew's porta potty, she'd not really heard anyone else complaining. "Weird? In what way?"

Greg shrugged. "I guess when someone's business is at stake, people go a bit crazy. Look at Ferdinand. He'll do anything to protect the show."

It sounded suspiciously to Ali like he was making excuses for Ferdinand's outburst, but something he'd said had started the cogs whirring in her mind. Suddenly, Ali was struck by a thought. She wasn't the only person who'd complained about the treasure hunters show after all. Shauna, the auburn headed woman from the pet store had been berating almost any treasure hunter that walked by that day. How had Ali failed to think of her as a suspect? She'd been so hung up on the idea that the killer was one of the treasure hunters motivated by greed or jealousy or revenge, she'd completely failed to consider the possibility of the killer being a desperate boardwalk vendor. And who was the most desperate? Who had the most to lose? Shauna! She had more reason to be annoyed than any other vendor on the boardwalk since her grand opening had essentially been ruined by the treasure hunters.

Ali's mind went into overdrive as she realized she needed to get back to Willow Bay as soon as possible. But Greg was still talking and she didn't want to be rude on top of demoralizing. The poor guy looked as glum as a kid with coal on Christmas.

"You know I heard a really funny rumor about that town," he was saying. "Apparently there's a demonic baker who makes voodoo dolls out of pastry!"

Ali's cheeks suddenly burned with embarrassment. That was it. Politeness be damned! She wasn't going to stand there and listen to yet another slanderous story about her. That was definitely her cue to get out of there.

She took a step back. "Heh. Sounds crazy. Anyway, I have to go now. Good luck with the search."

She backed away some more, as Greg glared at her with a confused, hurt expression. "You're leaving? But didn't you just drive all day to get here?"

"Yeah. I did." She laughed nervously, itching to get away. "And now I have to drive all day to get back! That's just how it is when you're an uber fan!"

She laughed again then turned and raced away before anyone said anything. The trip to Wave Bay had not gone the way she'd been expecting. But at the very least she was leaving with a new lead to pursue, one that circled her all the way back to Willow Bay, and the newest boardwalk vendor, Shauna, the pet store owner.

CHAPTER FOURTEEN

Ali drove at speed back the way she'd come, returning to Willow Bay in record time. She parked her car in one of the downtown lots closest to the end of the boardwalk where the new pet store was located, then hopped out of the car and raced out of the lot on foot.

She rounded the corner, her footsteps clattering on the wooden planks of the boardwalk, and she was temporarily blinded by the bright sunshine. But as the vision spots cleared, she halted, stopping in her tracks with astonishment as the strangest scene unfolded before her eyes.

There, marching out of the automatic glass doors of the pet shop was Shauna, the owner. Her auburn locks flowed behind her in the ocean breeze, and she had the darkest scowl on her face. In one hand, she was holding a knife.

Ali leaped behind a palm tree out of sight, her heart hammering with shock. What was Shauna doing with a knife?

Cautiously, Ali peeped around the trunk and spied the pet shop owner. She watched as the angry looking woman marched up to the inflatable dog and stabbed it with the knife.

Ali gasped and ducked back out of sight. Evidently, things with the pet store had not gone according to plan for Shauna, and she was taking her rage out on the inflatable dog. But seeing her with a knife like that, and seeing the amount of aggression and fury she'd levied (albeit at an inanimate object), didn't sit well with Ali.

Just then, Greg's words from the battleground echoed through her mind: *"I guess when someone's business is at stake, people go a bit crazy."*

How badly wrong had things really gone for Shauna, she wondered. Her grand opening had likely been ruined by the detectorists. Had she retaliated over it? Had she unleashed the same fury against Vincent Cole that Ali had just witnessed her unleash against an innocent, inflatable dog?

She gulped and mentally moved Shauna all the way up to the top of her suspects list. And now it was up to no one but Ali to question her. But how would she get the answers to her questions? She couldn't exactly walk in and start asking about her alibi for the night of the murder, could she? She would have to come up with some sort of plan. And she would definitely need to proceed with extreme caution. Shauna was holding a knife after all…

As she combed through her mind searching for a plan, Ali peeped back around the palm tree. She was just in time to see Shauna stomp back inside her store, leaving the inflatable dog behind her to slowly deflate on the boardwalk. Air gushed from the puncture wound she had so viciously inflicted upon it.

As it shriveled like a balloon, Ali spotted something behind it. It was none other than Scruff. The poor dog was barking with distress as his new inflatable friend melted before his very eyes.

"Poor Scruff!" Ali cried. He had grown very attached to the inflatable dog, and he looked confused and desolate to see it deflate.

Her heart lurched for him, and she felt instantly compelled to approach and offer him comfort. But she stopped herself, recalling how he'd failed to recognize her before. In her disguise, she was little more than a stranger. Approaching Scruff now, while his little doggy brain was busy trying to comprehend what was happening to his inflatable friend, might make a confusing situation even worse. She would have to make sure she showered him with affection later instead, when she was out of disguise and back to her familiar self. She could also give him his favorite Jumbo bone, as well, to help soften the blow of the untimely loss of his friend.

"That's it!" Ali cried, as an idea suddenly popped into her head. She'd just thought of the perfect ruse to go inside the store and speak to Shauna: she could go in to get Scruff a consolation Jumbo bone! Not only did the poor little stray deserve a treat, but it would give her the perfect cover story to start asking Shauna questions and digging for answers.

Emboldened by her plan, Ali left the safety of the palm tree and approached the pet store. Through the windows she could see Shauna inside, stomping around with a furious scowl on her face, grabbing things off the shelves and dumping them in a big plastic container storage bin on wheels. It looked suspiciously to Ali like she was packing up the store. But why would someone open a store one day and leave the next? Unless they were running away from something. Something like the local murder detective…

Ali shuddered with apprehension as the large automatic glass doors swished open, beckoning her inside. She steeled herself and stepped through.

A long, large aisle stretched before Ali. Parallel to it, she could see the auburn-haired woman's head bobbing up and down, disappearing out of sight then reappearing again. She was muttering angrily to herself, and loud thuds and thunks rang out through the otherwise empty store as she continued removing things from the shelves and dumping them in her wheelie bin.

Ali walked cautiously along the parallel aisle, closing the space between them. Shauna disappeared once again, and Ali leaned up on her tiptoes, peeping over the top of the shelves. Shauna was crouching down, grabbing items from the bottom shelf. The knife she'd been holding before was nowhere in sight, but that wasn't going to make Ali any less cautious. It might still be on her person, and there were plenty of other heavy-looking items around she could use as a weapon in a pinch.

"Excuse me, ma'am," Ali said, remembering at the last minute to put on her Midwestern persona. "Do you sell Jumbo bones?"

Shauna's head snapped up. Spotting Ali peering down at her, she scowled, then puffed her stray auburn bangs from her red face and stood, dumping the armful of items into the wheelie bin.

"*Jumbo bones?*" she said with a tone of disdain. "You feed your dog that trash? No. I don't sell Jumbo bones."

Ali grimaced. Shauna was even frostier than she had been when they first met. She couldn't help but wonder why she was being so rude to a potential customer. You'd think she'd be grateful for the business.

"Do you sell anything similar?" Ali asked.

Shauna flashed her a scathing look, her gaze roving up and down her polka dot dress. "I sell the finest quality food. The type that actually makes animals healthy. The sort of food fit for a pedigree. Do *you* have a pedigree?"

Ali grimaced again. Shauna was being more than simply frosty. She was being downright hostile! Ali sensed something was weighing on her heavily. A guilty conscience, perhaps?

"I don't have a pedigree," she said, trying to keep up her pleasant facade. "He's just a mutt. Nothing special. A farm dog, really. Helps keep the birds away from the corn."

Shauna's gaze had now found Ali's mud-caked sandals and her top lip curled with disgust. "Figures," she muttered.

Ali had dealt with some difficult people during her investigations to say the least, but to go from someone as creepy and unpleasant as Ferdinand to as hostile and rude as Shauna was really testing her patience. It was going to take herculean effort to keep her cool…

Shauna let out a long, weary sigh. "Come with me."

Ali clenched her jaw and followed the mean, judgmental woman through the aisles.

As she followed Shauna between the rows of luxury animal toys and state of the art litter boxes, Ali tried to think of ways to broach the subject of Vincent's murder without rousing any suspicion.

"Has your store been open long?" she asked Shauna's back as they walked.

"Nope, I opened yesterday. Huge mistake."

"A mistake? Why?"

"They're filming a show on the beach about treasure hunters. It completely overshadowed my grand opening."

"Oh, I'm sorry. That's such bad timing. You must be furious."

"Furious?" Shauna scoffed. "That's an understatement."

Just then, a flash of metal caught in the bright strip lights above. Ali noticed Shauna's weapon half tucked into the waistband of her pants. Not a knife, Ali realized now on closer inspection, but a pair of dog grooming scissors... Perhaps Ali's overactive imagination had simply filled in the blanks?

They halted by an aisle filled with beautifully packaged and eye-wateringly overpriced doggy treats.

"Here," Shauna said. "Peruse at your leisure." She turned to face Ali, but as she did, her gaze went over her shoulder and her eyes went suddenly wide. "You've got to be kidding me! It's that horrible dog again!"

Ali frowned with confusion and alarm as Shauna pulled the scissors from her waist band and started waving her fist over her head.

"Get lost, dog!" she bellowed, before shoving a sharp elbow into Ali's side to push her out of the way.

Ali staggered back, her back colliding with the shelf. "Ooof!"

But Shauna didn't seem to even notice. She marched away, waving the grooming scissors menacingly in her fist above her head.

For someone who ran a pet store, she seemed to really not like animals. Or customers. She'd been nothing but rude since Ali had stepped foot inside her store, and now she'd aggressively shoved her into the shelves. She was clearly unhinged!

Pushing herself off the shelves she'd collided with, Ali looked over to see what exactly had caused the furious outburst in Shauna. To her surprise and horror, she realized it was Scruff. The dog must have slipped in behind her when the automatic doors swished open! Now he had his entire head buried in a bucket of treats, and Ali's shock turned instantly to fear as she watched the furious Shauna advance on him, brandishing her weapon like a madwoman.

"I've had enough of you, dog!" she yelled.

"Scruff!" Ali cried, suddenly terrified that a raving murderous lunatic was about to harm him. "Watch out!"

At the sound of her voice, Scruff's head darted up to reveal a very tasty looking treat in his mouth. He locked eyes with Ali and tipped his head to the side curiously, as if he was trying to work out why this stranger had such a familiar voice.

"Scruffy, please!" Ali cried, desperately. "Run! She's going to kill you!"

Whether he'd worked out who she was or not, Ali didn't know, but he must have decided to trust her because he suddenly bolted for the door before Shauna could get to him.

The auburn-haired woman whirled around to face Ali. Her face was beet red with fury. "You thought I was going to kill the dog?"

Ali pointed at the grooming scissors in her hands. "I saw what you did to the inflatable outside."

"The inflatable isn't real! I only had permission to have it there for twenty-four hours, so it had to go. I would never harm a real animal." She put her hands on her hips, looking both furious and perplexed. "Wait. You called that dog by his name. How do you know him?"

"He's a local stray," Ali said.

"I know that. He spends all day standing outside the door, slipping inside with a customer and then stealing the food. What I want to know is how *you*, a girl who supposedly lives in a corn field in the Midwest, knows that."

Ali gulped. She'd been rumbled. In her fear over Scruff, she'd accidentally let slip who she was.

Suddenly, Shauna marched up to her and grabbed the straw hat straight off Ali's head. "I knew it," she bellowed. "A new hairstyle isn't going to fool me. It's you. The baker." She snatched the sunglasses from her face next, throwing them to the ground with a clatter. "What are you doing in my store in disguise? What game are you playing? You know I've heard a lot of rumors about you. I didn't believe them before, but now, after this, well, I don't know what to think."

Ali felt her heart pounding in her chest. Shauna was still holding the grooming scissors, and now she was getting even more riled than she had been before. What if Ali became her next victim?

She took a step back. "You've heard rumors about me? What rumors?"

97

"That you're a killer. Everyone says you killed Vincent."

Ali halted. *Vincent.* Shauna had called him by name. But she hadn't lived in town long enough to know his name, so how did she? Perhaps because she had been the one to kill him?

"How do you know his name?" Ali asked, keeping one cautious eye on the scissors.

"Same way everyone else does. I saw it on the news last night." She pointed at a small television behind her counter, which seemed to be tuned to a twenty-four-hour news program.

Ali's pulse spiked. Had she just found a hole in Shauna's story? Vincent had been killed *after closing time.* There was no way Shauna could have learned about the murder from the TV behind the counter because her store would've been closed for the night. She was lying.

"Last night?" Ali probed.

"Yes. Last night. I worked late," Shauna stopped as if suddenly cottoning on to Ali's questioning. "You can check the cameras if you don't believe me." She folded her arms. "And you? Where were you?"

"I was in my bakery."

"Do you have an alibi?"

Ali couldn't believe how terribly this was going. She'd come in here to find out if Shauna was the killer, and now the tables had been turned right back on her. Shauna was the one doing the interrogation of her!

"I'm not a killer," Ali said, firmly. "I have no motive to kill Vincent. Unlike you."

"Me? What motive do I have?"

"Your grand opening was ruined because of all the treasure hunters and the camera crew who came here. They were only in town because of him."

"And how exactly would killing him solve that problem?" Shauna cried. "Why would I murder one person when the whole beach is still crowded with treasure hunters?"

It was a very good point: one Ali had failed to consider. Vincent's death had done nothing but draw even *more* attention away from the pet store.

"Anyway, from what I've heard about you, you don't need a motive," Shauna said. "I heard you kill people just for the thrill of it. Get out! Get out, you murderer, or I'll call the cops!"

She was yelling loudly now and brandishing the grooming scissors again. The last thing Ali wanted was to give Detective Elton any ammunition to arrest her. Besides, she and Shauna had reached an impasse. Both accusing the other. Neither willing to back down.

With her tail between her legs, Ali scurried for the exit. As the doors swished open, she turned back and shouted, "I am not a murderer!" for good measure, then hurried onto the boardwalk.

As soon as she was away from the scary situation, she hung her head glumly. What Shauna had said actually added up. She didn't have a motive to kill Vincent. And by the sounds of things there was CCTV footage to back up the claim. Shauna wasn't the killer. And that meant Ali had hit a dead end.

She was about to trudge back to the bakery when she heard a bark. She looked over to see Scruff bounding toward her. He must have recognized her voice from before and now with her hat and glasses gone, he also recognized her again. He started running excited circles around her ankles.

"I'm so glad to see you," she said, bending down to pet him. "Oh! But Scruff. I still owe you a Jumbo bone."

Scruff barked and wagged his tail excitedly.

Ali petted him. "I take it I have my sidekick back now. Your friend is gone, and my disguise is basically ruined."

He barked again.

"Good," Ali said, staring out across the vast ocean. "Because I need all the help I can get. All my leads have gone cold." She looked back at her furry companion. "Come on. Let's go back to the bakery. Maybe Dad and Piper can help, too. If they haven't burned the place down, of course."

And with that, they walked away.

CHAPTER FIFTEEN

Seagulls circled overhead as Ali walked back along the boardwalk with Scruff.

She was frustrated to have hit another dead end and a little shaken up by her encounter with Shauna.

As she reached the little alcove, she cast her eyes over to the pizzeria, currently in darkness. It was crazy to think it was hers now, that it was sitting there empty, waiting for her to breathe life into it. Vincent's murder had really derailed all her plans and thrown a wrench in the works. The sooner she could solve the case the quicker she could get back to her life.

She pushed open the bakery's glass door, making the brass bell above tinkle.

Her dad was inside, sitting at a table with Piper. There were several empty coffee cups on the surface, along with several plates covered in crumbs and blobs of colorful frosting. It looked like the pair had helped themselves to a feast in her absence.

"Ali?" Piper exclaimed as she entered. "What happened to you? You look like you got all dressed up for a date but ended up being dragged through a hedge backwards!"

Ali glanced down at her ruined disguise. How was she supposed to explain this away, when her cover all day had been that she was buying organic almond essence?

"I passed a boutique in Wave Bay," she blurted. "I couldn't resist getting this new dress. It's cute, huh?"

"It's cute," Piper agreed, with a perplexed frown, "but the sandals...And your *hair?*"

"Alright, alright," Ali said. "I may have gotten a little sidetracked and walked through a field. And I don't know how to look after my hair because I always have it in a braid."

"Well I think you look beautiful," Richard jumped in.

"Thank you, Dad."

"I think you look beautiful too!" Piper cried defensively. "I mean, it's definitely a start. And kudos for trying. I always knew you could be really pretty if you put in a bit of effort. You just need to invest in a good conditioner."

It was a typically tactless comment from Piper, and Ali had to stop herself from huffing. Instead, she looked down at the detritus on the tabletop. "So… what have you guys been up to all morning? Stuffing your faces?"

"*Sampling* all your amazing goodies," her father amended. "And I must say, you are a very talented baker, Ali."

"Beautiful *and* talented?" Ali teased, putting a hand to her chest. "Stop, you're making me blush." She began to pick up the plates and stack them in her arm. "I take it that the shop hasn't been particularly busy today?"

"It's been totally dead," Piper said, before gasping loudly and putting a hand to her mouth. "No, not dead! I don't mean dead! No one's dead!" She laughed nervously. "I just mean that no one's been coming in because of the…," she mouthed the final word from behind her hand, "...murder."

Ali flashed her a withering look and shook her head. Piper had a tendency for putting her foot in her mouth, and she wondered how many times today her ditzy assistant had almost blabbed about the murder, how close she'd come to accidentally revealing the truth and sending Richard Sweet running for the hills. Knowing Piper, probably more than one.

Ali decided the best thing to do would be to get out of the bakery and as far from her dad as possible, or else run the risk of her talking about the murder and driving him away forever.

"You know," she said cautiously, "if there's no one coming in, then I think you should get down to the beach. See if you can catch the afternoon filming."

Piper's head lifted. "Really?"

"Sure," Ali replied. "If there's no one to serve, there's nothing to bake, and we don't need both of us on shift." Besides, after witnessing the terrible boss-employee relationship between Ferdinand and Greg, Ali would do just about anything to make sure she and Piper never ended up that way. Who was she to stand in the way of her young assistant's dreams?

"Are you sure?" Piper asked rapidly, jumping from her seat and beginning to hastily untie her apron strings.

"Of course," Ali said. "Go. Be free. Get that big break!"

Piper looked thrilled. She pulled her apron haphazardly over her head and dumped it onto the tabletop, leaving it in a crumpled heap as she hurried for the door.

"Thanks, Ali!" she cried as she threw the door open and halted on the threshold. "Do you still want me to come back for the hourly check-ins?"

"Yes please," Ali said. "Just in case things pick up. I mean, the treasure hunters seemed like caffeine fiends yesterday, so I don't really know why..." But her voice trailed to silence as she realized why no one was coming into her store today. All the rumors she'd heard while investigating on the beach pointed to *her* being the killer. There was no way any of the treasure hunters were coming to *Seaside Sweets* today, except for maybe the cynical old man who'd started the rumors in the first place.

"No problem," Piper said. "I can bring back some ice cream! Richard found this cool new ice cream parlor on the boardwalk. A retro one. It's made to look like a proper old ice cream parlor that sells all the traditional flavors. He keeps popping out to buy ice cream because it's *soooo* good."

"There are fifty flavors to try," Richard piped up. "Next on the list is vanilla cookies."

Piper nodded with childish glee. "We're trying to see if we can try all of them by the end of the day without barfing!"

Ali bristled. One of her fondest memories of her dad was their secret shared love of ice cream. Her mother refused to buy it for any of the kids, convinced the sugar would immediately rot their teeth. Highly strung Hannah bought into the fear mongering and Teddy preferred to satiate his snackish tendencies with chips, which left Ali and Richard as the only ice cream eaters in the house. Her father sneaking out to buy her a cone or two on a sunny Saturday when her mom was at her 'Buns of Steel' aerobics class had been one of the highlights of Ali's childhood. Hearing that he and Piper had essentially done the same thing behind her back rankled her.

Without meaning to, a dark scowl appeared above Ali's eyes. While she'd been busy running across muddy fields and getting insulted by treasure hunters and crazed pet shop owners left, right, and center, Piper and her father had seemingly been enjoying a delightful, carefree day. And they'd made quite the mess in the process.

She resumed collecting the plates, moving more quickly and less cautiously, making them clink loudly as she stacked them haphazardly on top of one another against her arm. As she lifted the final plate, she discovered a piece of paper on the table beneath it, with a handwritten list on it. Ali recognized her father's penmanship straight away from the many letters he'd written to her. But the list on the table was of ice cream flavors, and Ali realized from the check marks against some of them that these were flavors Piper and her father had tried so far. She couldn't help but feel frustrated that *this* was what her father had chosen to do with his morning.

"What flavor do you want, Ali?" Piper asked from the door.

"None. I'm fine. I don't really like ice cream all that much," Ali muttered.

Richard peered up at her with a frown. "Really? But you used to love it as a child. Do you remember our secret Saturday trips?"

"Not really," Ali replied evasively, adding the last plate to the stack in her arm.

She turned to head to the kitchen, noticing out of her peripheral vision the way Piper and her dad exchanged a worried glance between one another. They must have picked up on her demoralized mood.

"Okay, well, I'll be back in an hour," Piper said from the door, her tone now uncertain.

"Uh-huh," Ali replied.

The bell tinkled and the door clicked shut after Piper. Without looking back, Ali carried the heavy stack of plates across the shop floor and through the steel doors of the kitchen. She dumped the stack of plates into the sink, her heart slamming against her chest with a mixture of anger and hurt. She took hold of the countertop, forcing herself to breathe more deeply. This was all too much for her. The stress was becoming overwhelming.

Just then, she heard the swing doors flap open behind her and her shoulder tensed. Her father had followed her, clearly concerned about the change in her demeanor.

"Ali?" he said cautiously. "What's wrong?"

Without turning, Ali grabbed a cloth and disinfectant spray, and channeled her emotions into cleaning the counters, using big, aggressive sweeping gestures. "Nothing."

"Yes it is. I can tell. Something is bothering you."

"The bakery needs cleaning, that's all. Piper seems to have forgotten about hygiene. Maybe all that ice cream gave her brain-freeze..."

Suddenly, Richard's hand pressed down onto her shoulder. Ali stopped what she was doing as he squeezed it with gentle reassurance.

"Ali," he said in a soft, tender voice. "I'm your father. Whatever's going on, you can tell me."

With a sigh, Ali turned to face him. She desperately wanted to believe that she could tell him anything, that he would help her because he was her father. But the truth was he had not been there for years. She'd gotten used to solving all her problems on her own.

She gazed into her long-lost father's eyes, words failing her. How could she tell him she was embroiled in a murder investigation? That everyone down to the local detective thought she was a psycho killer? It would send him running for sure. *Again.* She simply couldn't risk it.

She exhaled sadly, the cloth and disinfectant spray falling limply to her sides. "I can solve my problems on my own." She turned back to the counter and started wiping again.

But her dad was clearly not about to give up that easily. "Is it the expansion?" he pressed.

Ali let out a noise from the back of her throat. If only that was all she had to worry about! "No. It's not that."

"Oh, because I thought maybe you'd want to see this…"

She halted with curiosity and turned back. "What?"

With a cheeky grin, Richard held out a piece of paper to her.

Ali took it and glanced down. It was the same piece of paper with all the ice cream flavors listed on it. "I don't understand."

"Other side," Richard told her.

Ali flipped it over. On the back of the paper was another list. Not ice cream flavors but several different local traders—carpenters, plumbers, plasterers, even landscape gardeners. Next to each one was a telephone number and a price, and at the bottom of the paper all the figures had been added up to a grand total.

"What is this?" Ali asked, glancing up at Richard.

"I haven't just been eating ice cream all day," her father replied with a chuckle. "I did some research. Chatted with some traders. These are the ones I got the best impression from, and who also gave reasonable quotes after a bit of negotiation. There are a couple of slightly more expensive ones, but I thought these would be the best compromise."

Ali was taken aback. She was touched he had gone to the effort for her. And guilty to have been so cross before...

"Dad…," she stammered, feeling her lip tremble as if on the verge of tears. "You did this for me? Why?"

"I want to help," Richard told her.

Ali felt a wave of gratitude. It was the sort of work she usually balked at. She didn't understand how traders worked, or how to negotiate with them, and she always ended up feeling like she'd been short-changed. It was why she often enlisted Teddy to help with financial negotiations, as she had for the rent at the store. It was also why she had installed the bakery's sink and oven all by herself with the help of how-to videos on YouTube.

"I have a lot of lost time to make up for," Richard added.

She looked up from the list in her hands. "Thanks, Dad. I really appreciate it." Things had been strained between them since Richard had shown up and it was a relief to feel warmth toward him.

She looked down at the sum at the bottom of the page. "But I don't know whether I can afford to hire all of these people," she added. "That's a lot of money and—"

"I'd like to pay," Richard blurted.

Ali's eyes widened with astonishment. She didn't know what to think about that, or how to even begin processing what he'd just said. Surely her father couldn't afford to pay for the work. He'd lived in a van for the last sixteen years, for Pete's sake; surely he wasn't in a financially stable position. And he'd only just re-appeared into her life. She didn't want him to make a huge financial contribution just out of guilt.

She looked up from the note, shaking her head. "I can't ask you to do that."

"You're not asking. I'm offering."

She hesitated. "But I don't even know what I want to do with the pizzeria yet."

"We can figure it out together. Using my plans, Delaney's plans, and your ideas."

Ali's reticence grew. It wasn't just about the money now. She felt pushed. Her mind was too focused on the investigation to properly think about the pizzeria. "Both your plans are great," she said, "but I don't know if either of them is exactly what I want. A restaurant seems like a lot of effort."

"I sampled every single one of your goodies today," Richard said supportively. "You're talented, Ali. Really talented."

"At baking, sure," she said with a self-conscious shrug. "But owning a bakery and a restaurant are very different things. I don't know if my skills could transfer."

"Of course they could! You have the talent. The training. The business acumen. And with my investment, you could definitely make it a success. Ali, I have no doubt you would make an exceptional restaurateur!"

Ali wished she could believe him, but in her mind's eyes she kept seeing flashes of *Eclairs,* the fancy French restaurant she'd worked at in LA. She hated it there. From the clientele to the whole vibe of the place, she just wasn't a restaurant kind of girl. And if her father had been in her life during the three terrible years that she'd worked at *Eclairs* he'd already know how much she hated it.

"It wouldn't suit my personality," she mumbled.

At that moment, Richard finally seemed to realize his offer was being refused, and he deflated, his chest visibly sinking. Ali pressed her lips together. The last thing she wanted to do was offend him, especially since he was clearly trying so hard.

"I'll think about it," she said, folding the paper and slipping it into her back pocket. "And thank you. Truly."

At the sound of her sincere gratitude, Richard seemed to perk up again. "Good. Now. Let's talk about Vincent Cole."

Ali froze, thrown immediately for a loop. "You... you *know?*" she stammered. "About the... the..."

"... the murder?" Richard interjected, finishing the sentence she was struggling to. "Yes! Of course I know about the murder! Did you really think you could keep it from me?" he tutted.

Ali tensed. Her heart started to pound. Had Piper let slip after all? Was her father about to run for the hills, away from the dangerous town, away from her?

"How did you find out?" Ali asked, her voice small.

"I saw the cops on the beach when I first went to buy ice cream," he explained. "As soon as I got back, I asked Piper what was going on. She told me everything."

Ali's shoulders slumped as she sighed. Of course Piper had told him everything. Her assistant couldn't keep a secret, even when Ali had explicitly asked her not to speak about Vincent's murder when she had phoned her from the battleground in Wave Bay.

"Why did you hide it from me?" Richard asked.

Ali squirmed uncomfortably. She felt seven-years-old again. "I didn't want to worry you. I didn't want to scare you away."

Richard's face fell with understanding. His voice dropped. "You thought I'd... leave again if I found out?"

Ali nodded. "I thought it would be too much of a burden."

"Oh, Ali," Richard said through his exhale. "Your problems aren't a burden. And I'm not going anywhere. I'm not going to leave you. Again."

Ali felt her bottom lip tremble. She'd been worried about him finding out and abandoning her again, but her fear had been unfounded. Her sometimes macabre life wasn't going to drive him away. He wanted to stick around this time. She needed to start trusting him that he would.

"I'm sorry I didn't tell you," she said. "I'll be more honest from now on."

Richard gave her a smile. "You know, Piper told me about all the other cases you've solved. About how smart you are. How strong and independent."

"She did?" Ali replied, coyly, feeling her cheeks warm.

"She speaks highly of you," Richard said. "So, am I right in thinking you were in Wave Bay following up the lead on Ferdinand rather than buying almond essence?"

Ali's eyebrows flew up with astonishment. How did her father know about Ferdinand? She'd only learned about him herself from the cantankerous old man on the beach! "How did you guess?"

"Because I have a bit of a penchant for sleuthing myself," Richard told her.

He smiled, broadly. Ali found herself returning the gesture. It pleased her to think she might have inherited her curious mind and sleuthing skills from him. It was better than having inherited just his temper, that was for sure.

"I've come up with a few theories," Richard continued, pulling a notebook from the pocket of his cargo shorts. "Want to see?"

Ali eyed the thick, ring-bound notebook as he flipped through several pages of scrawled notes. She felt guilty for her earlier frustrations about him spending all day evaluating ice cream flavors and eating all her cupcakes. It seemed that her father had actually been using his time rather wisely, and helpfully. "What is all that?"

"Theories."

She was astonished. Her leads may have all gone cold, but perhaps her father had an idea she'd not thought of yet. "Come on then. Let's get a coffee and I'll take a look."

They headed out of the kitchen to the bakery floor. Ali poured them both a coffee, then father and daughter settled down at the window table to brainstorm about the case. Together.

CHAPTER SIXTEEN

Ali had no idea how long they spent sipping coffee while going through Richard's notebook, because they both shared the same habit of becoming so thoroughly engrossed in their activity that they lost track of time. It was only when the bell over the door tinkled that either of them broke their deep concentration.

They looked over at the door in unison as Delaney and Seth came inside.

"Hey guys…," Ali said, a little confused to see them. Delaney often stopped by for coffee and chats, but Seth hardly ever ventured this way. He was far too busy running his successful gourmet hot dog restaurant to visit her lowly bakery. "What are you doing here?"

"Piper told us about your dad," Delaney said, softly. "We came to see if you were okay."

Was there anything Piper hadn't blabbed about? Ali wondered. Then she gestured across the table to Richard. "Ta da. Delaney, Seth, this is my father. Dad, these are my friends, Delaney and Seth."

"Oh!" Delaney exclaimed. She'd obviously not expected him to be literally in the bakery sitting opposite her when she entered. She held out a hand to shake. "Richard. It's great to meet you."

"Ali's told us lots about you, sir," Seth added.

Richard shook their hands in turn. "It's a pleasure to meet you, too. I must say, you make quite a handsome couple. You remind me of me and my wife when we were your age."

"They're not a couple!" Ali exclaimed, embarrassed on their behalf. "We're all just good friends. Delaney runs the craft store and Seth makes gourmet hot dogs." She felt bad for them as they exchanged an awkward look.

"What's all this?" Seth said in a somewhat obvious attempt to redirect the conversation. He was looking down at the pages of scrawled theories.

"Dad and I are brainstorming theories about who killed Vincent Cole."

"I knew it!" Delaney cried. "I knew you'd be investigating! That's what the disguise was for, wasn't it?"

"Yes," Ali confessed. "And it worked. I got a pretty strong lead. But it ended up being a bust. Now all my leads have gone cold. It's a dead end. Hey, do you guys want to join us? Put all our heads together? I'll give you free coffee and cakes for your troubles!"

Delaney and Seth exchanged another glance. It was as if they'd been expecting to find a very different Ali at the bakery than the one bouncing around excitedly in front of them. Ali couldn't really blame them. They had both heard her woefully complaining about her missing father and probably thought the shock of him turning up had sent her a little bit cuckoo.

"I mean… Carys *is* covering the restaurant," Seth said.

"And I've closed for lunch anyway," Delaney added.

"Perfect!" Ali cried.

She hopped up from her seat, feeling more energized than she'd anticipated. It definitely wasn't from the caffeine, which she regularly drank by the bucketful, so the only explanation was that she was drawing her energy from her father's support. It was a peculiar feeling to Ali. Her mom was never particularly supportive of anything she did— the bakery and her habit of getting involved with murder investigations being right there at the top of her grievances. Hannah was like a second mother sometimes in her disapproval, and Teddy was like the great gay surrogate father she'd never had, but it just wasn't the same. Ali had always had a calm, quiet, understated confidence inside of her, but now her father's support seemed to have banished the voices of doubt that often bounced around inside her skull.

As Delaney and Seth took their seats beside Richard, Ali went to the counter to pour them all coffee, listening to the three of them making awkward, stilted chatter.

"You two seem to have come up with a lot of theories," she heard Delaney say. "What does 'alien guy; mean?"

"He's a detectorist," Ali called from the counter. "He has a weird thing about aluminum. We thought that might have been the motive."

Richard coughed. "That was perhaps one of our more fanciful ideas."

"What about 'druid ceremony?'" Seth added.

"Ah, that one is a bit less out there," Ali said, returning to the table with the tray of coffees. She began passing them out. "There are quite a lot of shaman types with dowsing rods. They don't seem to be treasure hunters at all. We wondered if they might have done some sacrificial ceremony or something, because of how greedy everyone is these days.

Something like that." She sat back in her seat and cupped her hands around the steaming coffee cup left over for her.

"You're being... thorough," Delaney said, clearly choosing her words very carefully.

"We don't want to leave any stones unturned," Richard said.

"Only problem is, none of our theories have any leads," Ali added.

Seth rubbed his dark, stubbled chin contemplatively with a hand. "Did you try the pawn shop?" he asked, fixing his dark brown eyes on Ali.

"The pawn shop?" she said, frowning. "No. Why would I try there?"

He shrugged. "I figured if someone killed Vincent for the coin, then wouldn't they try to sell it? It's not the sort of thing you'd want to keep in your pocket. Especially not with the police around. The pawn shop is the only place in town to get rid of something like that."

"But pawning it would be too risky, wouldn't it?" Delaney chimed in. "There are police everywhere."

"Risky, sure," Seth replied. "But it would be worse to be caught red-handed with it jangling around in your pocket! In my humble opinion, anyway..."

The cogs in Ali's mind began whirring as she let Seth and Delaney's exchange percolate in her mind. Then she glanced up at him and gave him a decisive nod. "Seth's right. Kind of." She addressed the three of them sitting around the table as she explained. "If the killer has any sense, he'll try to get rid of the coin as soon as possible. To exchange it for money. But I don't think he would do it at a pawn shop. Pawn shops send regular reports to the cops to make sure they're not dealing with stolen goods."

"Really?" Richard asked.

Ali nodded. "I learned that from Detective Callihan." She felt the blush rise in her cheeks and quickly fought to suppress it.

"So how would the killer have sold the coin?" Delaney asked. "If not at the pawn shop?"

Ali pondered the question. "He must have found someone else to sell it to. A dealer who specializes in coins, for example."

"The antiques store!" Seth cried with sudden vigor.

Ali paused, tipping her head to the side as she considered his suggestion. "Antiques store? There aren't any in Willow Bay, and I don't think he'd be able to leave town without the cops noticing. They're on high alert."

"There is," Seth contested. "An antiques store. In Willow Bay."

Ail blinked at him curiously. This was news to her. "There is? Where?"

"On the boardwalk," Seth said.

"Where?" Ali exclaimed with disbelief. She had been to every place on the boardwalk, or so she thought.

"It's tucked out of the way a bit," Seth explained. "Easy to miss. But it's there. I promise. I've been inside."

A spark of excitement flamed in Ali's chest. If there was an antiques store in Willow Bay. then there was a good chance the killer had sold the gold coin before Vincent's body had even been discovered. It was a good lead, and one Ali was eager to pursue.

"Seth, you're a genius!" she exclaimed, jumping up from her seat.

She motioned for the door, only to halt in her tracks when it was opened and Piper entered, returning from her trip with delicious-looking ice creams in her hands.

"Perfect timing," Ali said, looking from her assistant to her father. "I need you two to cover the store again. Ice cream dream team back in action. I have a new lead I want to pursue."

Richard looked skeptical. "The antiques store? Really? It's not a great lead..."

Ali put her hands on her hips. "Maybe not. But it's the only lead I've got."

Richard shook his head. "I disagree." He gestured to their notes. "Any one of these theories would be better to pursue. All we'd have to do is ask around on the beach and..."

"—you're forgetting something very important," Ali interrupted. "I already did ask around. No one wants to talk to the locals. The animosity seems to go both ways. I only got lucky because that one old guy seemed to hate the young detectorist crowd and sided with me as the lesser of two evils."

A tense silence fell around the table. No one seemed to know where to look, as if they were frightened Ali and her dad were about to launch into a full-blown disagreement. Which wasn't the case at all. This was just friendly banter as far as Ali was concerned. They should have seen her when she was eighteen and he'd missed her graduation...

"Okay, okay," Richard said relenting. "You go to the antiques store. Piper and I can handle the bakery."

Ali wasn't so sure leaving the two of them in charge was such a good idea considering they had spent all morning eating cupcakes and drinking coffee, but if there weren't many customers coming in anyway because they all thought the bakery was owned by a murderer, then it didn't make too much difference who was manning the place. May as well be them. That would free her up to follow the new lead.

"Great," she said.

"Just come straight back once you realize it's not a lead," Richard added.

Ali gave him a look. "Alright, Dad. And I'll even let you say, 'I told you so.'" She motioned for the door.

"But Ali, what about your ice cream?" Piper said, holding up the most delicious looking cone filled with creamy scoops of raspberry.

"You can have it," Ali said. "Add it to your list."

"But I've already tried this flavor."

"Then give it to Seth and Delaney!" Ali exclaimed. "There'll be time to try ice cream after I've solved this murder."

And with that, she hurried away, feeling reinvigorated by the new lead.

CHAPTER SEVENTEEN

As soon as Ali stepped out of the bakery, she heard the welcome sound of Scruffy barking. She glanced along the boardwalk and saw her favorite furry fellow come bounding toward her. He was wagging his tail eagerly, as if he already knew they were off to follow a lead, and Ali grinned down at him as he reached her and wound himself around her legs. She was grateful to have her sidekick with her for this portion of the investigation. With her team of sleuths back at the bakery and her canine companion at her heels, Ali felt like the solution to Vincent's murder was now well within her grasp.

"Come on, Scruffy," she told the pup. "We're looking for an antiques store."

They headed along the boardwalk, scanning the store fronts for the elusive antiques store. Ali still didn't understand how there could be a place on the boardwalk she'd never been to and had never even heard about. She was very familiar with the boardwalk and all the vendors because she'd been their unofficial spokesperson during a town meeting about taxes. How she failed to notice an antique store was a mystery.

Just then, Scruff barked to alert her. Ali paused to see what he had found. "Is that... no way... it can't be... you've got to be kidding me!"

She paced forward peering up at the thoroughly underwhelming small wooden building. It was barely more than a shed, and rather dilapidated looking. It was painted a boring off-white color and there were streaks of years-old seagull poop streaking the windows. The sign read: *Jimmy's Antiques.*

"No wonder I didn't know there was an antiques store in Willow Bay!" Ali proclaimed. Among all the colorful and unique stores and eateries on the boardwalk, the antique store's drab exterior had never really grabbed her attention. She must have walked past it a hundred times and assumed it was just another one of the disused beach huts that dotted the boardwalk.

She looked at Scruff. "Good job finding this place. I probably would have missed it if you'd not been here to point it out. But... I can't take you inside. Antiques stores sell very expensive and often breakable objects."

Scruff sat back on his haunches and tipped his head to the side as she spoke.

"You do understand, don't you?" Ali asked him.

With a nasally-harrumph, Scruff settled down on his front paws, indicating he was begrudgingly going to wait it out.

"There's a good boy," Ali said, and she opened the door of the antique's store and headed inside.

Straight away, Ali was struck by an unsettled feeling. Over the door instead of a normal brass bell, there were several wind chimes dangling down. Despite her five-foot-two statue, she had to duck not to hit them, and as she closed the door behind her they chimed discordantly, making her even more uneasy.

She peered into the poorly lit store. There was no air conditioning inside, and the smell of dust and mildew was rather overpowering.

"Hello?" she called.

Her voice was met by complete silence. It didn't seem like anyone was around. No customers. Not even a clerk.

Ali slowly began to peruse the shelves. The shop was stocked with the most random selection of artifacts, things she could never imagine anyone actually buying. It almost seemed like the stock was just a bunch of items left behind on the beach. There were parasols and buckets for making sandcastles nestled among a million different beach towels rolled up into a colorful display. An array of woven sun hats was on display next to several stands full of sunglasses. There were even some nice designer ones, Ali noted. But a few designer pairs of sunglasses and some elegant hats weren't really enough to detract from the general lost 'n' found, bric-a-brac vibe of the place. Perhaps she'd spoken too soon when she called Seth a genius. This was less an antiques store and more of a thrift store. An antique coin would stick out a mile in a place like this.

With a huff of disappointment, Ali was about to turn around and leave when she heard the sound of shuffling coming from a back room. It sounded like footsteps. The store clerk must be on his way to her.

A moment later, an old, stooped man appeared in the threshold of the doorway holding a cane.

"Thought I heard someone out here," he said in a croaky, aged voice. "What are you looking for, dear?"

"I already looked; you don't have it."

"Are you sure? I have most of everything. Bucket? Spade? Hat?"

She shook her head. "No. I was looking for a coin," she told him. "A gold one."

114

The man's demeanor instantly changed. His eyes flashed with sudden fury. "Ahhh, you're one of *them,* aren't you? One of those treasure hunters?" He narrowed his eyes with cold, hard fury.

"I'm local," she began to explain but the old man didn't seem to hear her. Instead, he was waving his cane about like he wanted to hit her with it!

"I'll tell you what I told the rest of them!" he cried, throatily. "I don't want your business! I don't need your money! And I certainly don't need your disdain!"

He started swishing his cane threateningly, and Ali had to step back to avoid it.

"I'm not a treasure hunter!" she exclaimed, holding her hands up. "I'm a local."

But it was no use. Either the man was too old to hear her, or too angry to. He clearly hated the treasure hunters, and while his reaction was rather extreme, Ali couldn't really blame him. They were hardly an ingratiating bunch. They'd given her a hard time over a thirty second delay for a coffee, after all, so who knows what this doddery old man had had to put up with from them?

"Get out!" he yelled. "Out, out, out! If you're going to turn your nose up at my stock, then you'd better go to that flashy Thiago's!"

He sneered the last word and Ali's curiosity piqued.

"Thiago's?" she asked. "There's another antiques store in Willow Bay?" Perhaps that was the one Seth had been referring to? If there was another store, that would explain a lot. She couldn't understand why he'd send her to this bizarre place!

"Not Willow Bay!" the old man snapped. "Haven Bay! Haven Bay!"

He glowered at her like she was an imbecile. But at least he had actually *heard* her that time. And he'd stopped waving the cane, so that was progress.

Ali spoke with caution, not wanting to set him off into a rage again. "I'm sorry if I offended you," she said. "I'm a local vendor. I run the bakery. I've never even heard of Thiago."

The old man's eyes narrowed. He blinked at her. "Never heard of him?" he asked, and Ali spotted a hint of triumph in his expression.

"Nope," she said, running with it. "Who is he? He sounds... *flashy.*" She echoed the man's own language back at him to make it seem like they were in agreement. It seemed to work.

"Thiago is a ruthless man who's going to ruin my business," he explained. "We both do the same thing, sell lost items from the beach.

Only he's incredibly competitive. Any time there's a valuable find, Thiago will go to any lengths to make sure he gets it for his own store."

"Any lengths?" Ali echoed, wondering if murder may be one of them.

The old man nodded. "He can get aggressive. He's been squeezing out all the competition along the coast for years. It's just me left now, and I'm only surviving because I make sure I go for the stuff I know he won't want. The towels and sunglasses and things. If it's anything worth over a hundred dollars, I leave it for him. It's not worth the aggravation. He knows to leave me alone now."

"That sounds awful," Ali said, sympathetically. "He sounds like a bully."

"He is. He was on that TV show the other day, shouting at someone in front of a crowd."

"*Antiques Hunters?*" Ali asked, her interest in this ruthless antiques hunter mounting.

"I don't know what it's called. They've been filming it on the beach. The man has a terrible haircut, like a rockstar!" He shook his head and groaned in a curmudgeonly way. "What ever happened to short back-and-sides?"

Ali nodded, though she was barely listening anymore. The old man had set the cogs in her mind into overdrive. She needed to find out more about this man, Thiago.

"Well, I can see you're very busy here," Ali said, backing away toward the door.

"Aren't you going to buy anything?" the old man demanded.

"Not today. I'll be back, for sure!" And with that, she ducked under the wind chimes, making them ring discordantly as she raced out the strange store and back onto the boardwalk.

Back out in the fresh ocean air and bright sunshine, Ali found her heart was actually racing. Her visit to Jimmy had been rather strange to say the least, and she was going to have some choice words to say to Seth when they next met up! But at least she had gotten a potential lead out of it.

Scruffy jumped up from where he was sitting by the door and ran to her.

"Good news," she told him, taking her cell phone from her pocket. "I have a new lead."

She went online and straight to the *Antiques Hunters* website where she found their short video section. With a spark of embarrassment, she realized the video of her confronting Vincent was one of the top links, titled *Crazy Baker Throws A Fit.* But just below it was another. *When Antiques Hunters Lock Horns.* She clicked on the link and the familiar Willow Bay beach filled her screen.

Sure enough, it showed a tanned man in suit shouting at Vincent Cole, claiming ownership over the coin.

"You can't just take things off the beach!" he was yelling.

Which was rich, Ali thought, considering that was exactly how he made his living.

She watched the video, determining that Thiago's fight with Vincent couldn't have happened that much after her own confrontation with him. Mullet Man seemed to be buzzing with malevolent glee that he'd caught *another* heated altercation on film, and even Ali had to admit it made entertaining television when it didn't involve her...

Decisively, Ali exited the screen on her phone and put it back in her pocket. She looked down at Scruff. "I think you and I ought to visit Haven Bay."

He barked a yes, and they headed off to get her car.

CHAPTER EIGHTEEN

Ali put the pedal to the metal and drove with speed and determination along the coast to Haven Bay. In the passenger seat beside her, Scruff sat alert and eager, watching the beautiful coastline of golden sands and sparkling blue oceans whizz by with rapt attention.

When her little car passed the *Welcome to Haven Bay* road sign, Ali gave a gasp of surprise by just how opulent the town was. The stores that lined the main road were high-end: a collection of delis, boutiques, and jewelry stores. Gold letters stuck on the inside of the window of a hairdresser's proclaimed: *only organic ingredients used* along with a list of eye-wateringly high services in the same gold writing.

Ali couldn't help but compare it to Wave Bay, the town the other way along the coast from Willow Bay. She'd visited it following an incorrect lead for her father and had found the place fancy and snooty. But now Wave Bay seemed practically backwater in comparison to Haven Bay!

"Even the palm trees look expensive!" Ali exclaimed to Scruff, as she peered through the windscreen with awe. It looked as if they'd been grown from a special rare kind of seed! Either that, or Haven Bay had its own ecosystem!

Up ahead, Ali spotted a sign for an underground parking lot and headed straight for it. She followed the spiral curve down to the lower level and parked up, then took the stairs up to the beach with Scruff trotting up alongside her.

"I'm glad you're here," Ali told him as they climbed the staircase toward the bright, salty smelling sky. "No offense to your inflatable friend or anything…"

Scruff barked happily. He'd probably already forgotten the friend he'd made—and subsequently lost—outside the pet store.

The pair emerged from the lot at the boardwalk. Here, Ali noted, was more of the same: extremely luxurious stores selling everything from expensive watches to cashmere sweaters and homeware; ornate palm trees that appeared to have been sculpted rather than grown; and not even a single bit of stray trash blighting the scene. It was like being in a parallel universe version of Willow Bay, Ali thought. Perhaps one where the councilor's proposed boardwalk taxes had actually passed and run all the businesses away, leaving only high-end luxury brands to be able to afford the rents? She shuddered at the thought of this imagined alternative future, then bowed her head, and marched on.

As Ali scanned the store fronts looking for the antique store, she'd come here for something else caught her eye. A sign for a *Patisserie,* or, in other words, a bakery. The competition…

Ali couldn't help herself. She halted. She was just too curious for her own good sometimes and took a step closer to evaluate the bakery.

Scruff stopped beside her ankles and peered up at her curiously as her gaze roved all over the exterior of the bakery, assessing it. Pretty woven flower baskets full of luscious, bright purple flowers hung invitingly either side of the glass doorway, which was rimmed with brass and had a large push bar handle, just like the Parisian cafés she frequented during her training in France.

She spotted the menu in the window and took a step forward. The bakery was also a restaurant, she discovered, serving breakfasts, lunches and dinners, along with baked goodies all throughout the day. Breakfasts included croissants, pan eu chocolat, French toast, and cinnamon rolls. Lunch was a selection of quiches, croque monsieurs, and savory tartes. Dinner diverged from the cold pasty offerings and was more in line with traditional French bistro cuisine—escalopes, boeuf bourguignon, and steak frites.

Ali couldn't help the pang of jealousy that spiked inside of her. Apart from the dinner menu, the bakery was selling everything she'd originally hoped she could sell in the bakery. Her plan at the outset had been to use her extensive French pastry training to sell all manner of goodies, before she'd quickly learned the people of Willow Bay were simply not interested in that type of fare. So she'd switched to cookies and cupcakes. The only time she really flexed her culinary muscles was with her range of famous rainbow macarons. And as much as she adored her bakery and her work there, she felt a sudden stab of jealousy for this *patisserie* that had achieved what she'd wanted and failed to.

It was also very busy inside. She could see through the window that every table was occupied. So not only was this bakery thriving with a menu more closely aligned to her original plan, but it was also busy during a time that her own was suffering because of the murder investigation.

Ali sucked her teeth and rocked back on her heels, torn between heading inside to check it out more, or getting on with what she came here to do—solving a murder. In the end, she decided that lining up for a croissant to-go while quietly scoping out the competition wouldn't delay her too much.

"I'll be right back," she told Scruff, then she pushed open the door and went inside.

Sweet smells of fruit, cream and pastry wafted into her nostrils straight away, but Ali felt the vibe inside was totally wrong for a seaside eatery. It had been decorated to resemble a Parisian café, with round wooden bistro tables and a large wall mirror. It had a serious, somber vibe. Servers in tight, buttoned-up white shirts walked around with dour expression, delivering coffees and cakes to the seated customers on round black trays perched on their fingertips beside their ears. The whole place reminded Ali of *Eclairs*. It couldn't be further from her own bakery, which was quaint, calm, relaxing, bright, and fun.

A server approached her, a dark-haired woman with bright red, heart-shaped lips and a striking combination of black eyeliner and bronze shimmering eyeshadow. She handed a menu toward Ali.

Ali shook her head. "No thanks. I'm just getting something to go."

The server pointed toward the counter. "Then you need to be in *that* line," she said, in a tone as brusque as her makeup was dramatic.

Ali bristled at her impoliteness. "Thank you."

She paced over to join the back of the line for the take-out counter, wondering what the manager would do if they knew how rude their staff were. She certainly wouldn't tolerate that kind of behavior from Piper. For all her faults, Piper was charming to the clientele, and they loved her for it.

Ali joined the back of the line, glancing around the man in front of her so she could see into the glass cabinet. There were lots of fancy French desserts on offer—cream-filled profiteroles and glazed madeleines—the types of things she'd originally planned on making at *Seaside Sweets* before she realized the Willow Bay residents and tourists preferred the simple treats like cupcakes and cookies. Ali wondered whether the fancy desserts really were well-liked by the customers here, or whether they were just props, status symbols and signifiers.

She reached the front of the counter where a tall woman with dark gray hair held back into a tight ponytail stood waiting for her, her expression severe and impatient. Ali's eyes fell, automatically, to her name tag. *Sabrina. Manager.*

"Oh! This is *your* restaurant?" she exclaimed before her brain had even engaged.

Sabrina the manager looked down her thin nose at Ali, her lips pinched. "Yes." Her tone was dry and suspicious.

"I run a bakery," Ali explained quickly. "In Willow Bay. Maybe you've heard of me. *Seaside—*"

"—*Sweets?*" Sabrina replied with little interest. "Yes. I've heard of you."

Her tone was so cold, Ali became suddenly flustered. She'd been nothing but polite and friendly to Sabrina so far and yet the woman hadn't even raised a smile. She didn't know what to make of the severe looking Sabrina or her comment. She'd already heard of *Seaside Sweets*? How? In what capacity? As the beloved bakery from the next town over, or as the bakery run by the demonic witch who made voodoo dolls out of pastry?

Ali fought her instinct to ask *how* Sabrina knew her, because she got the distinct impression the answer would be something she'd prefer not to know...

"I'll just take a croissant," Ali said, her voice small.

Sabrina tonged a croissant from the display cabinet and slid it into a paper bag. "Three-fifty."

Ali's eyes widened. "Three-fifty? Three dollars fifty? For a croissant?" She'd not actually meant to blurt it out loud, but the eye wateringly high price had boggled her mind.

Sabrina glowered at her. "It's a traditional recipe. I studied in France."

Ali just managed to stop herself in time from exclaiming that she had *also* studied in France and that she *also* made croissants with the traditional recipe, but was still inclined to charge her customers less than half of the extortionate price Sabrina felt entitled to...

"Then I suspect it will be the best croissant I've ever eaten," she said instead, keeping her tongue firmly in her cheek as she exchanged money for the paper bag containing the croissant.

She scurried away, wondering how such a snobby, rude, over-priced place was so full of clients.

As she emerged back onto the sunshiny boardwalk, Ali thought back to her father's suggestion that she should run her own restaurant. Maybe he was right? If Sabrina could run such a successful restaurant in spite of her unpopular, over-priced menu and rude staff, then surely Ali could run a successful restaurant with polite, friendly staff and a tasty, appropriately priced menu? Maybe she'd been selling herself short, just like her father had insinuated?

Just then, her phone dinged with an incoming message. She checked the screen. It was Piper.

"Why are you in Haven Bay?" the message read.

Ali remembered the Track My Friends app and rolled her eyes as she pictured her dad, her assistant and her friends all sitting together in the bakery watching her every move.

She quickly typed back. *'The antiques store was a dead end. But I got a new lead that led me to Haven Bay.'*

She hit send, only for her phone to immediately begin flashing with an incoming telephone call. This time, it was the *Seaside Sweets* landline calling her. She answered the call.

"Piper? Is that you?"

"Ali, this is your father," came Richard's voice.

The unexpected sound of his voice in her ear startled Ali. She realized then that the last time she'd spoken to her father on the phone had been when she'd screamed at him for missing her high school graduation. The memory caused a sudden wave of anguish inside of her.

"What is it, Dad?" she asked.

"I'd like to know why you're in Haven Bay," he said.

Ali rolled her eyes. "I literally just texted Piper about this. I'm following a lead. I'm going to an antiques store called *Thiago's.*"

"Why? I thought we agreed the killer would not have risked leaving Willow Bay to sell the coin?"

"Well the weird old man Seth sent me to told me something interesting. *I* wasn't the only person who argued with Vincent on the beach before he was killed. Thiago did as well. If you get Piper to go on the *Antiques Hunters* website, there's a video of them arguing."

There was a pause on the other end of the line. "Ali, I'm not so sure about this. It sounds dangerous. You were supposed to collect leads, not go and confront a potential killer on your own."

"I'm not on my own," Ali assured him, looking down at Scruff. "I have Scruff. Besides, you and Piper are following my every move on that app! Trust me. I'm not a teenager anymore. I can handle this."

There was another hesitant pause. Then finally, Richard sighed. "I trust you. Stay safe."

"I will," Ali replied.

She ended the call and with a surge of determination, headed off in search of *Thiago's.*

CHAPTER NINETEEN

"Here it is, Scruff," Ali said as she peered up at the antique store. Its facade was typically fancy for the area, and very different from the wooden shack Jimmy owned in Willow Bay. But if everything the old man had told her about Thiago's ruthlessness was true, then the huge disparity between their respective stores made total sense.

Just then, Scruff began to whine. Ali looked down at him. There was a look of concern in his chocolate, brown eyes.

"Not you, too," she said, crouching to pet him reassuringly. "Nothing bad is going to happen to me. I promise. I'm going to be okay." She pointed at the large glass door to the store. "Look, you can watch me through here, okay? If anything bad happens, bark your head off. Got it?"

Scruff peered at the door, his eyebrows twitching with skepticism. Then he walked over and took up position beside the door, sitting straight-backed and self-important like a guard on duty.

"That's my boy," Ali told him.

She went to open the door but halted. Despite all her reassurances to Scruff, her dad and Piper, she had to admit she was actually quite nervous about coming face to face with Thiago. If he *was* as awful as she'd been told, and if he *had* killed Vincent as she suspected, then she was about to put herself in a very dangerous situation. She would have to proceed with extreme caution and be extra careful with her cover story.

She took a deep breath to steady her nerves, then pushed the door open and went inside.

Thiago's antiques store was a world away from the one she'd left in Willow Bay. It was a vast space with high-vaulted ceilings, bright and airy like a museum, with light-colored tiles on the floor and sparklingly clean glass display cabinets. The items inside and on the shelves had clearly been very carefully curated. Instead of mismatching plastic buckets and spades, there were beautiful pieces of jewelry on display. Some seemed to be bespoke pieces made of rare gems, and Ali wondered what sort of people lost their expensive jewelry on the beach.

She reached a display cabinet full of wedding rings and felt a mournful pang in her chest for all the people who'd lost such a sentimental item on the beach. Surely Thiago had dealt with more than a few unhappy people in his time, discovering their precious, lost jewelry on display in his store. But then maybe that was where he got his ruthless reputation from? And perhaps that was why his store was so markedly different from the one in Willow Bay? Where Jimmy felt enough pity for the people who'd lost their jewelry that he'd return it to them, Thiago would keep it and the riches for himself. If that were the case, it was certainly building up an interesting picture of the type of person Thiago might be in her mind. The type of person who killed someone else for their riches…?

She paced inside further, glancing all around her. This was the perfect place for a rare coin to fit in.

Just then, she heard the sound of footsteps clicking on the polished tiles coming toward her, and her breath caught in her throat as she turned to see a man in a smart, dark blue suit approaching. He was tall, with golden-hued skin and long, light brown hair tied back into a ponytail. It was definitely the same man from the video, the one who'd argued with Vincent Cole on the beach of Willow Bay, demanding he hand over the gold coin to him.

He halted beside her, hands clasped behind his back, holding himself with a self-assured confidence that practically oozed from him. "Greetings," he said with a nod. "How can I help you today?"

His appearance and overly polite manner were so unexpected, Ali had to check his name badge to double-check he really was Thiago. She'd expected him to be burly. Brutish. But not only was he none of those things on the surface, there was also no hint of them lurking beneath his exterior. Ali shuddered as she considered the very real possibility that Thiago was wearing a mask of civility to cover up a monster lurking beneath.

It took Ali a moment to remember her backstory. She put on a moneyed accent, channeling the sort of nonchalant narcissism she'd seen Ferdinand exhibit back at the battleground.

"I'm a buyer for a wealthy gentleman who collects coins," she said, lazily, as though spending vast sums of money on valuable coins was a daily occurrence for her. "I've been told you have the best coin collection in California, and I've come to see it."

Thiago smiled, though Ali noticed that it did not touch his eyes.

"Of course," he said. "Please, come with me." He gestured toward a large glass display counter, showing off several sparkling gold rings on his fingers and a heavy-looking gold watch on his wrist.

Ali tried not to react to his overt display of wealth, instead simply looking past him to the cabinet. She walked over, her shoes clicking on the polished tiled floor, and peered into the cabinet.

It was filled with antique coins, each one displayed individually in a way that reminded Ali of butterflies in a museum. Beside each was a small plinth of text explaining what it was and why it was worth the eye-wateringly high price written on the tag.

Ali scanned across all the different coins on display but none of them was the Spanish coin she was searching for. Suddenly, it occurred to Ali that if Thiago was the killer, he probably wouldn't put the gold coin on display so soon after the murder. He'd have to be stupid to do that. From the vibes she was getting off him, he was far from stupid.

"Mm," she said, straightening up. "These are nice. But not what I was led to believe you sold. Do you have another collection? A special one?"

Thiago regarded her for a long moment. "Who did you say you were a buyer for?"

"I didn't," Ali said. "And I won't for privacy reasons. Let's just say money is no object."

Thiago's lip twitched at the side. This appeared to be the right thing to say. His eyes darted left and right, then he leaned in and lowered his voice.

"I do have some other coins," he said, conspiratorially. "Recent acquisitions I'd prefer not to put on display."

Ali's heart bounced in her chest. Recent acquisitions? That sounded very promising. Could this be it? Was Thiago about to show her the gold coin Vincent Cole had been murdered for?

"Show me this other collection," she said, boldly, fighting to keep her trembling nerves out of her voice.

"Certainly," Thiago said. He gestured toward an arch in the wall on the other side of the room. "This way."

Through the arch, Ali could see only darkness and she swallowed nervously. If she went through the arch, Scruff wouldn't be able to see her through the window anymore. He was her first line of defense. Without his watchful eye, she felt vulnerable.

"Can't you bring it to me?" she tried.

Thiago regarded her with his forced-polite expression, clasping his hands behind his back once more. "The items in the next room are photosensitive. Due to their age, I have to make sure they're kept in the darkness, so they remain in perfect conditions. I'm sure you understand."

125

Ali hesitated. She didn't know what to make of the explanation. It sounded suspicious to her. She knew antique paintings and documents could get damaged by exposure to sunlight, but she had no idea coins could. Was Thiago spinning a yarn? Had he cottoned on to what she was doing? Or was the answer to Vincent's murder lying just beyond, in that dark, shadowy room?

There was no other option, Ali decided. She would have to follow Thiago through the arch into the dark unknown beyond.

She stole a quick glance at Scruff waiting on the other side of the door, then turned back to Thiago and forced her voice to sound calm. "Then please lead the way."

CHAPTER TWENTY

As Ali followed Thiago across the shop floor towards the ominous looking arch, all the worry Piper and her father had expressed before suddenly made sense to her. This situation was taking her far outside of her comfort zone. It had the potential to spiral very quickly out of control. She was about to follow a suspected murderer into a dark room, alone, without even her dog as backup.

"Mind your step," Thiago said as he went through the arch. "It will take your eyes a little while to adjust to the light."

Ali swallowed the lump in her throat and stepped into the darkness.

Immediately, she felt very disoriented. The room reminded her of the dark room in her high school's photography lab, with a peculiar red glow. It smelled similar too, like strange chemicals.

"Embalming fluids," came Thiago's voice from somewhere nearby.

Ali jumped a mile. "I'm sorry?"

"The smell. It's embalming fluids for the taxidermy. I heard you sniff and assumed that was why."

"Right. Yes," Ali said. This guy was scarily perceptive. It only made her feel more disconcerted. "So, may I see the coin now?"

"Of course. Here."

She felt a wooden tray being pushed into her hands and glanced down. In the dark red light of the room, it was very difficult to see what she was looking at. But as her eyes finally adjusted, she was able to see the small collection of gold coins inside.

She squinted with confusion. The coins all had the same motif on them, the Canadian maple leaf.

"This isn't what I was looking for," she said.

"Oh?" Thiago replied, sounding thoroughly confused. "But you asked for my most recent acquisitions. I can assure you they're genuine. 99.99% pure gold."

Ali didn't know what to make of this but there was one thing she knew for certain. These coins had *not* been found on the beach. People didn't just casually carry around pure bullion gold coins. How Thiago had come into possession of them, she didn't know, but she got the distinct impression it was through underhand means. Stolen? Traded? She couldn't be sure. But something was definitely not right. She had stumbled into something she had not anticipated, something way over her head. The hairs on the back of her neck prickled and the instinct to get out at all costs overcame her.

"This isn't what I want," she said again. She shoved the tray back at Thiago and turned, heading for the escape route beneath the arch and the light beyond.

"Wait!" came Thiago's voice, following behind her. "I don't understand. If you're not here for the Maple Leafs, then what are you here for? Who are you?"

His tone had turned suspicious, and Ali hastened her step. She made it to the shop floor, blinking in the reassuring brightness, ready to beeline for the exit. But Thiago caught up with her. He grabbed her by the shoulder and turned her to face him.

"Who are you?" he demanded. "Who do you work for?"

From somewhere outside, Ali heard Scruff bark. Her furry protector could see her through the window again, and the clever perceptive dog must have worked out simply from Thiago's body language that she was now in danger.

"I'm no one," Ali stammered, trying to break free from Thiago's grasp.

But suddenly, a look of recognition flashed behind his eyes. His stare became penetrating. His face started to grow red. "Wait..." he said. "I know who you are. You're that bakery lady from Willow Bay! The one who got into a fight on TV!"

Ali gulped. Coming through the glass door behind her, Scruff's barking grew more feverish, and was joined by the sound of his claws scraping against the glass.

"What is this?" Thiago yelled, backing her into a corner. "Who are you working for? What trick are you playing?"

He was furious, and Ali felt entirely at his mercy. "I'm not playing a tr—trick," she stammered.

"Did Jimmy put you up to this? Ferdinand? Whatever you're playing at, don't think for a second that you're going to get away with it! I'll make you pay, just like I did with Vincent."

Just then, Ali's back collided with a display cabinet with a hard, loud thud. She threw her hand out behind her, grasping hold of the first thing it landed on. She pulled it out and brandished it at Thiago, only to discover she was holding a very flimsy looking antique wooden cuckoo clock.

"Get back!" she cried, waving it around in front of her.

Thiago's face cracked into a sneer. "What are you going to do with that?" he scoffed.

Ali wasted no time. She threw the cuckoo clock right at his face, hitting him square between the eyes.

"OW!" Thiago cried, doubling over.

Ali didn't waste another second. She bolted for the door, her feet pounding against the marble tile floor as her heart thudded in her chest.

But just as she reached the exit, the door flew open so fast the bronze bell above let out an angry jangle. A figure thundered inside, moving so rapidly Ali was flung to the side. She fell, landing on the hard polished ground.

Suddenly, Scruff was there beside her, sniffing and barking. He must have run inside with the strange figure.

Ali's head darted up, and she looked through the straggles of blond hair that had fallen over her eyes at the stranger who'd rushed inside and was now heroically grappling Thiago to the ground. To her surprise, she recognized who it was right away. It was none other than Detective Callihan!

"Sebastian!" Ali cried, as a spark of electricity went through her. She couldn't quite believe her eyes. She'd never been more happy to see him than she felt at that moment.

The detective turned, locking eyes with her. "Ali?" he cried with astonishment. "What are you doing here?"

"What are *you* doing here?" she cried.

"Making—an—arrest," he struggled to say while Thiago bucked and writhed beneath him. Finally, he clicked the cuffs in place. "Thiago Fernado, you're under arrest on suspicion of illegal gold coin trading."

Suddenly, Ali heard more footsteps at the door and turned to see, this time, Detective Elton came running in.

"Callihan?" the female detective cried as she assessed the scene before her with her hawkish eyes. "What are you doing here?"

Detective Callihan hauled Thiago to his feet. "I'm arresting our main suspect in an illegal gold bullion fraud scheme." He frowned at her with confusion. "What are *you* doing here?"

"I'm meant to be arresting him for murder!" she exclaimed.

Just then, Thiago's eyes widened with shock. "Murder? I...I didn't kill anyone!"

Ali's mind spun from the speed of everything that was happening. Seeing Sebastian had sent an almost euphoric jolt of relief through her. But seeing Detective Elton had doused the flame almost immediately, because she couldn't help but suspect that the only reason she was there was because she'd been following her.

"Let's get him down to the station then," Detective Callihan said. "Read him his rights."

Detective Elton nodded, but she seemed a bit miffed to have been beaten to the punch by her partner. Especially considering he was supposed to be working a completely different case to her.

She looked at Thiago. "You're also being arresting on suspicion of the murder of Vincent Cole, okay?"

"But I didn't murder anyone!" Thiago cried again, protesting profusely.

"Save it for the station," Detective Elton said.

Sebastian bundled him out the door, with Detective Elton following behind. Ali pulled herself out of her crumpled heap to her feet and staggered out the door after them, an anxiously whining Scruff keeping close to her ankles.

"Miss Sweet," Detective Elton said, looking over her shoulder at her and stopping her in her tracks.

Ali gulped. "Yes?" She was half expecting her to admonish her for throwing a cuckoo clock in a man's face like a weapon. Perhaps even use it as an excuse to arrest her.

"Let me remind you, once again, that you need to leave police business to the police," Detective Elton said.

"Yes, detective," Ali said.

And with that, the detective gave her a curt nod and turned away, getting into her car. Meanwhile, Sebastian shoved Thiago into the back of his car. Then both cop cars drove away.

Ali watched them, stunned by everything that had just transpired, trying to piece together. It seemed that Thiago had been the prime suspect on the two separate investigations the detectives were working on — Detective Elton's case on the murder of Vincent Cole, and the case Detective Callihan had been transferred to, which seemed to be nothing to do with shady black market criminal gangs as Ali had feared, but fraudulent bullion gold coin trading.

She wondered how long Detective Elton had been waiting around outside the store, leaving Ali in a dangerous situation inside before Sebastian had intervened...

"I guess that's it," Ali said to Scruff, petting his head. "The bad guy's going to jail. Which means you and I can go home."

He barked happily, recovering from his earlier anxiety. They headed back to the parking lot together.

But as Ali got into her car, she couldn't help but feel like something wasn't quite right. There was a nagging doubt in the back of her mind about Thiago being the killer. Something that didn't sit right with her.

She shook her head to get rid of the feeling. It was probably her brain trying to come up with more reasons for her to avoid the inevitable conversation with her dad that now needed to take place. But if she could survive everything she'd endured over the last few days, then she could certainly handle what he was about to tell her. And then she would be able to finally get her life back to normal.

She grabbed her phone, seeing a stream of worried texts had come in from Piper while she'd been otherwise occupied in Thiago's store. She quickly texted back.

'I'm okay. The bad guy's been caught. What flavor of ice cream do you guys want?'

With a smile, she slid her phone back into her pocket and began to drive home to Willow Bay.

CHAPTER TWENTY ONE

The beach was still full of treasure hunters when Ali drew up outside the brand-new ice cream parlor.

She studied the exterior. The store was so new it didn't even have a sign above its door yet. But it did have a cute pink and white striped awning outside to provide shade, and some pretty hanging baskets filled with white flowers. Through the window she could see glimpses of the vintage interior Piper had been raving about.

She looked down at Scruff standing protectively beside her ankles. "You know the drill, boy," she said. "No coming inside the shops. *Unless* you think I'm about to get murdered, in which case it's perfectly fine."

Scruff barked his acknowledgement, and Ali smiled at the memory of him pawing at Thiago's door when she was in danger, before bounding in to check on her the moment the door opened. Her smile widened as her memory continued, reminding her of the surprising moment Sebastian Callihan had burst inside and heroically grappled Thiago to the floor. Not only was the murder case solved, so too was case that had kept Sebastian away from her for the last few days. Life was about to return to normal with the added bonus of Sebastian Callihan being back in it. Perhaps they could continue where they'd left off, with that promised proper first date...

Suddenly, Scruffy barked, and it pulled Ali out of her swooning daydream and back to reality.

"Sorry," she said with a coy blush. "I'm getting distracted..."

The dog settled into his soldier-on-duty position by the door and Ali headed inside the ice cream parlor with a renewed spring in her step.

Straight away she could see why Piper and her dad liked this place so much. It was just as they'd described, a Victorian era ice cream parlor combined with a drug store and a barber's shop. It reminded her of the old feel-good black and white movies she'd seen as a kid. The walls were exposed red brick, the floor dark green and white checkerboard tiles, and in one corner was a proper antique leather barber's chair. There was a large gold framed mirror attached to the wall, surrounded by rustic looking, dark wood shelves filled with dusty old amber glass pill bottles and a gramophone as decoration. There was even a price list, and Ali realized then that the barber's shop was not just for show; it really was offering the service.

It was exactly the sort of quirky, unique business that would not have been able to open in Willow Bay if the proposed tax hike had passed. Ali had fought hard against it, to make sure small, independent stores could continue to make the boardwalk their home. Her efforts had paid off, and here was the evidence. This cool, quirky, unique ice cream-parlor-come-barber's-shop!

Proud of her accomplishment, Ali approached the register.

By the look of the man standing behind it, he was just as committed to the whole Victorian aesthetic as he was to the decor. He was wearing a black silk waistcoat over a white linen, buttoned shirt, and had a designer beard that stretched across his cheeks in intricate curls and twirls. He even had mutton chops like a character from a Victorian novel. His high, arched eyebrows gave him a somewhat perplexed expression.

"Now, let me guess," he said in a throaty voice. "You're here for a hot towel shave?"

Ali smirked. "Actually, I'm thinking of growing out my moustache."

The man chuckled good humoredly at her quick wit, and Ali took it as a good sign. Not everyone appreciated the Sweet siblings' particular brand of sarcasm, and she was glad this new neighbor seemed more chill than grumpy Shauna at the pet store.

She tapped her fingers on the counter, rocking on her heels. "Actually, my dad and assistant have been raving about this place. Now I've finally gotten the chance to come in, I can see why."

The man beamed with pride, making either side of his gelled moustache quiver. "Thanks, that's nice of you to say. So what can I get for you?"

"One second," Ali said, reaching for her cell phone in her pocket. "I have a list." She checked her phone to see what orders Piper had texted to her and was surprised to see that it wasn't just her dad and assistant who'd put in requests, but Seth and Delaney, too. So both of them were *still* at the bakery waiting for her to return? Were they all really that worried about her? Admittedly, she *had* just had a run in with a gold coin stealing murderer, but they were all acting a little over the top as far as she was concerned...

"Ready?" Ali asked the man, flashing him a sheepish grin.

"Hit me," the man replied.

Ali read from the screen. "One chocolate mint, one butterscotch, one salted caramel, one black forest gateau and one...." Her voice trailed off. "Oh you've got to be kidding me." She looked back up at the ice cream seller and added, wryly, "One crème brûlée."

The man gave her a peculiar look, one dark brow arching up. "I take it you're not a fan of crème brûlée?"

Ali laughed. "I have a complicated history with crème brûlées."

"Say no more," the man replied with a chuckle, and he went over to retrieve the metal ice cream scoop from a small bucket of steaming water.

Ali watched as he began to scoop the first ice cream in a very neat, practiced manner. It was quite mesmerizing to watch, hypnotic even, and Ali found her mind wandering back to her experience in Haven Bay.

With the murder investigation over and Thiago in police custody, a space seemed to have opened up in her mind and she found herself dwelling on the trip to Sabrina's Patisserie.

The place had been bustling, but disappointing, and it made her realize how much more within her grasp opening a French style restaurant was for her. Could she really do it? With her dad's investment and architectural know-how? Or would taking on such a huge task with the father she barely knew be a recipe for disaster? So far they had worked harmoniously side by side. But baking cupcakes and transforming an entire pizzeria into a patisserie were two very different things. And what about staff? She'd have to employ more people to cover the register and wait the tables and cook the food. Sometimes he felt like she'd taken on more than she could handle with just Piper. How could she really cope with the added responsibility of managing *more* staff? Especially if they were like Piper!

Just then, Ali was pulled out of her reverie by the ice cream man handing her the first cone across the counter, the chocolate mint flavor she had ordered for herself.

"Ta da!" he announced.

"Wow," Ali replied, as she took the beautifully presented cone. It contained a perfectly round, creamy brown scoop of chocolate ice cream, set neatly inside a wide, chocolate rimmed cone.

She took a lick, her taste buds sparking to life at the perfect combination of rich chocolate, and sharp mint.

"That's incredible!" she murmured through her mouthful. "The best ice cream I've ever tasted."

The ice cream seller smiled proudly, "Thank you." Then he dunked his scoop into the warm water again and got to work on the next cone, the butterscotch flavor her father had ordered.

"So you said your dad and assistant are fans?" he said as he worked. "Is that the pretty young lady with the blond hair who comes in once an hour, and the man with the cargo pants by any chance?"

"That's right!" Ali exclaimed, pausing mid-lick with delighted surprise. "How did you guess?"

"They're my most loyal customers," he replied. He handed the butterscotch cone over the counter, his expression falling. "To be honest, they're my only customers."

"Oh," Ali said, feeling a surge of sympathy in her chest as she took the second cone in her spare hand. "I'm sorry to hear that."

The man got to work on the next ice cream, Delaney's black forest gateau, his mood noticeably lower now. "I'm not sure what I'm doing wrong. I opened the parlor two days ago, and things haven't exactly gotten off to the flying start I was expecting. Maybe the prices are too high? People around here might be too stingy to pay for proper quality ice cream."

Ali hadn't actually considered how much it would cost her to buy five ice creams. She'd been on too much of a high over Thiago's arrest and the case being over to even think about it. She peered up at the chalkboard menu behind the man's head for the first time.

She almost choked on nothing when she saw the prices. Each scoop was *eleven dollars*! No wonder he was struggling for clientele when there were so many Mr. Whippy trucks on the beach selling ice cream for 99 cents! She dreaded to think how much Piper and her father had spent over at this place in their quest to try all fifty flavors. This was the sort of luxury Ali simply could not afford. Unless, of course, she started a thriving patisserie business...

She addressed the ice cream seller. "From one vendor to another, I'll admit your prices are on the higher end of the scale. *But* that's not to say the customers aren't there. I'm pretty sure the tourists will love the whole Victorian aesthetic and the barbershop and the old school recipe. People like spending money when they're on vacation."

He handed her the black forest gateau. "But I want to be appreciated for my art," he lamented as and moved on to make Seth's salted caramel. "This town seems to be populated with uneducated fools."

As she awkwardly juggled the three ice creams in her hands, Ali grimaced at the ice cream seller's rude comment. When she had first

135

started speaking to him, she thought he seemed nice and funny. But his attitude had quickly turned into an arrogant, condescending, woe-is-me attitude. He'd called the inhabitants of her beloved town stingy and uneducated. Two insults in as many minutes were *not* a good ratio.

"Okay, that's the salted caramel," he said, handing the fourth cone to Ali. "Last one, crème brûlée."

The final ice cream was Piper's order. Ali suspected she'd made it as a cheeky little call back to her monotonous crème brûlée making days at *Eclairs*.

"Do you want brûlée brittle on it?"

Remembering how Piper and her father were trying to sample everything on the menu, Ali nodded. "Yes please. That sounds good."

She glanced across the display counter at several silver trays lined up containing a variety of interesting looking toppings from fudge cubes to chocolate shavings and sugared nuts. She spotted a golden sheet of pure, hard brûlée brittle, like thick amber glass made of sugar. Just looking at it gave her a toothache.

As the moustachioed man picked up a small hammer and chisel to carve off a piece of brittle, Ali had to admit the parlor really was fantastic. She felt silly for having been so childish before when Piper was telling her about this place. She could see now why they'd liked it so much, and wished she'd joined in with the excitement rather than rejecting it out of jealousy. The ice cream man was very committed to his craft, and she liked the over-the-top theatrics of it all. Even the hammer he was using was aesthetically in keeping, with a beautiful wooden handle curved in an ergonomic way.

Perhaps she'd been too quick to judge. She had had similar thoughts as him when she opened her bakery, frustrated that the locals weren't sophisticated enough to appreciate her overly fancy French desserts. It had been disappointing to learn that the tourists and locals preferred simple cupcakes, but as soon as she had switched to give the people what they wanted, her business had thrived. She'd found success so quickly she now had the opportunity to create the patisserie of her dreams. The ice cream man would simply have to learn the same lesson too.

"You know there might be another reason why things haven't picked up yet," she said, deciding to be more generous to Willow Bay's newest, struggling vendor. "They've been filming a TV show down on the beach. I think it's been a huge distraction."

Straight away, the man's shoulders tensed. His dark brows inclined downwards, and he clenched his jaw so tightly, his gelled moustache quivered. "Yes. I spoke to the pet store owner, and she said the same thing. Her grand opening was overshadowed by the whole stupid treasure hunter debacle going on down on the beach just like mine was. We opened the same day. Talk about bad timing."

"You and Shauna opened the same day?" Ali asked. "That is bad timing. You know, I never asked, what are you going to call the store?"

"Mr. Moon's," he replied, and he lay the hammer back down on the brittle.

'Moon...' Ali thought, as a latent memory started to stir from the recesses of her mind. *'Moon...'*

Her gaze fell to the hammer Mr. Moon had put back down, and she spotted something that made her blood run instantly cold. There in the handle of the hammer was a strikingly familiar shape: the shape of a crescent moon.

A tremor went through her body. Sudden flashes of memories replayed in her mind of the murder weapon laying on the sand beside Vincent's body, with the same crescent moon image illuminated in the red, blue and white lights of the cop car.

She shook herself. She was being silly. A crescent moon design wasn't exactly uncommon or unique. Plenty of people felt an affinity with the moon, even going so far as to tattoo the image on their body. It was the same design but that was simply just a coincidence. What motive would the ice cream seller have to kill Vincent Cole?

Ali's mind turned over and over as Mr. Moon handed her the final cone, Piper's crème brûlée with the jagged piece of brittle sticking out the top.

"That will be fifty-five dollars all in," he said, seemingly oblivious to the panic that was now sweeping through Ali, causing cold sweat to bead on the back of her neck.

Ali's hands shook as she negotiated the five cones in her hands while also getting money out her pocket. She handed the note to him, and he turned to the register—an old brass one, of course, to fit the 1950s parlor aesthetic.

As soon as he was distracted, Ali's gaze darted all around the store, looking for something, anything that might exonerate the ice cream seller, anything to quell the suspicion flying through her mind. But now it seemed that everywhere she looked, she saw the same crescent moon shape she had seen on the murder weapon lying next to Vincent Cole. It was on the branded napkins wrapped around the cones. On the back of the barber's chair. On the chalkboard above it.

Then, with a sudden feeling of dread, Ali's gaze fell to the shelf beside the barber's chair...

There lay a set of beard-cutting tools. One of which was the perfect replica of the knife Ali had seen lying beside Vincent Cole's body on the beach. The same curved wooden handle. The same fold out implements. The same pokerwork burnished, half-crescent moon design.

That did it for Ali. Suddenly, she knew without a single doubt in her mind that she was in the presence of Vincent Cole's killer.

The voice of Greg from the battleground sounded in her inner ear. *"I guess when someone's business is at stake, people go a bit crazy."*

Just like that, all the pieces fell into place in Ali's mind. The pet store and the ice cream parlor had opened the same day, and both had been overshadowed by the descent of the detectorists and the TV crew to the town. But while she had guessed the right motive for the murder, she had attributed it to the *wrong* person. It wasn't Shauna from the pet store who'd turned a knife on Vincent Cole, blaming him for ruining her grand opening… it was Mr. Moon!

Just then the loud, sharp-metallic sound of the antique register's drawer slamming shut wrenched Ali out of her anxious ruminations with a gasp. She tore her gaze from the barber's shears and looked back to the counter. The ice cream seller was standing in front of her once again, only now, the expression on his face had completely changed. It had gone cold. Hard. Suspicious.

Ali gulped and watched as his gaze slowly and deliberately trailed over in the direction of where hers had previously been, landing on the barber's shears and the crescent moon burnished pokerwork in its handle. Then, in the same slow, deliberate way, he looked back at Ali and pinned her to the spot with his dark, penetrating, ice-cold glower. His face twisted into a knowing scowl.

There was no doubt in her mind now that he had seen what she had seen. That he knew she knew he was the killer.

And with a shudder of abject terror, Ali watched as a small, sinister smirk twitched the side of his lips upwards into an expression of murderous intent.

CHAPTER TWENTY TWO

Ali's heart pounded against her breastbone, so hard it felt like it could break a rib. She staggered back, her eyes glued to Mr. Moon standing behind the counter. He had the most terrifying, eerie expression on his face that Ail had ever seen. The transformation that had come over him was disconcerting, and Ali had no doubt he wanted to harm her, to tie up the loose end and do away with the witness.

"You look like you've seen a ghost," he said, his earlier conversational tone replaced by a cold, emotionless one.

His voice struck Ali like electricity, making icicles sweep up her spine. She wanted to run, but in her profound state of sheer terror, she found herself frozen to the spot, no longer able to move, to run, to scream for help.

The five ice creams she'd been holding suddenly fell from her useless, trembling hands. They splattered across the checkerboard tiles in an array of colors.

"Uh oh," said Mr. Moon's strange, terrifyingly cold voice. "Butter fingers. Let me clean that up." He snatched a cleaning cloth from the counter and went to walk around the counter.

That did it for Ali. Suddenly, her frozen limbs unlocked themselves, freeing her from the statue fear had made her. She whirled on the spot and went to run for the door.

But in her haste to escape, she trod on the puddle of ice cream from the cones she'd dropped. The sandals she'd borrowed from Delaney had no traction and she slipped and slid across the sticky puddle until she lost her balance and went tumbling to her knees.

As she crashed down onto the checkerboard tiles, her hands automatically jutted out to break the fall. They slammed onto the hard ground and an unpleasant noise like a twig snapping rang out. Ali felt absolutely no pain, but she knew, instinctively, that the sound was one of her bones breaking.

She floundered on her hands and knees, and caught sight of Scruff through the glass door, pawing and scratching at it, barking feverishly just as he had done at Thiago's antique store earlier. Only this time, he was directing all his attention on the handle. He must have worked out from watching Detective Callihan earlier what a door handle was for, and was now jumping at it, trying to push the handle so he could rescue her.

Ali gasped. Hope was not lost yet. If Scruff could just get that door handle open...

Too late. A sudden, dark shadow appeared on the tiles in front of Ali's hands.

Fear lodged in her throat. She turned to look over her shoulder and saw Mr. Moon now looming over her.

She stared up into his eyes. His pupils were so dilated his eyes had gone completely black, as if he had no irises at all. It gave him a demonic quality, making him look like an animal about to attack its prey.

Shivers peeled through her body as she realized he must have looked at Vincent the same way. He must have seen the man as a lesser animal that needed to be eliminated. A cockroach to be squashed beneath his heel. For all her thoughts earlier about Thiago wearing a mask of civility, she had been completely fooled by the ice cream seller's friendly veneer. But now she could see what he truly was. A stone-cold killer.

"I've heard all about you..." he said as he looked down at her. "You're the baker. The one who sticks her nose in everyone's business. The one who thinks it's her job to solve crimes." He reached into the pocket of his apron. "Well, not this time."

In one quick movement, he pulled his hand back out of the pocket of his apron and held it high above his head to reveal he was now holding a knife.

Ali's eyes went round with terror, and her throat became instantly dry.

"You d—don't have to d—do this," she croaked.

"Don't I?" Mr. Moon said, toying with the knife in his hands like it was a plaything, and this was all some sick, twisted game. "You mean if I let you go

you won't immediately go running to your detective boyfriend to tell him everything?" He twisted the blade under the lights, making it glint and flash. "You must think I'm an idiot."

He laughed demonically and Ali shivered all the way down to the bone. All this time the rumors had been about a demonic baker, when really it was the demonic ice cream seller everyone needed to worry about!

"Please," she cried, holding her hands up. "Killing me won't solve anything. It will only make everything worse for you."

"Maybe," he said with a shrug. "Or maybe it will make me feel better. Killing Vincent did. And I got a shiny gold coin for my troubles."

"You're—you're crazy!" Ali cried as it sunk in what exactly she was dealing with here. A deranged man. A knife-wielding lunatic.

And she was cornered. Helpless. There was no way out. Nowhere to run. Nowhere to hide. Her time was finally up. After all the risks she'd taken in the past to solve crimes, after all the times she'd danced with danger and put herself in harm's way in the pursuit of justice, *this* was where it ended, in an ice cream parlor at the hands of a crazy moustachioed psycho-killer.

But just as her hope faded, everything suddenly changed.

In a split second, too fast for Ali to comprehend, she felt a sudden gust of warm ocean air blast her from behind. Mr. Moon's gaze darted over her shoulder and his eyes widened with shock. Then something furry whizzed past her ear, soaring over her shoulder while emitting a low, deep growl. A split second later came a blood-curdling roar of pain.

Ali's mind swirled as quickly she put all the pieces together. The door to the ice cream parlor was wide open. Scruff had managed to work the handle and had pounced, teeth bared, straight over her shoulder, latching his jaw heroically around the arm Mr. Moon was holding the knife in.

Ali's heart soared as she watched the ice cream seller stagger back, roaring in pain, as he tried to shake the determined little dog off of his arm. But it was no use. Scruff's jaw was locked like a vice, and the knife Mr. Moon had been seconds away from plunging into her fell from his hand. It clattered to the ground before skidding across the tiled floor, sliding beneath the counter, and disappearing from sight.

If there hadn't been a myriad of other sharp implements within reaching distance, Ali might have taken a breath of relief. But with the barber's shears lying on the shelf just several feet from the spot where Mr. Moon stood, yowling in agony as he tried to shake Scruff off his arm, there was no time to relax.

Moving at lightning speed, Ali scrambled to her feet. She catapulted toward the open door and shouted "HELP!" at the closest passerby.

The man stopped and turned to look at her. Ali's heart instantly sank when she realized who it was. It was none other than the very first detectorist she'd met on the beach, the rude man who had insulted her and Scruff.

"Help?" he said with a scoff. "You? As if." Then he flashed her a disgusted expression and kept on walking.

A feeling of desperation overcame Ali. She looked around, searching for anyone else who might be able to help her. But she was interrupted by the sound of a terrible bark coming from behind her.

She whirled around, looking back inside the ice cream parlor. She'd never heard such a bark come from Scruff before and it had struck terror right into her heart. She was just in time to see a blur of fur slide across the checkered tiles at speed and crash into the opposite wall.

"Scruff!" Ali cried, her heart lurching with anguish.

Mr. Moon had successfully shaken the dog off. He stood free and unimpeded in the middle of the room. But he looked shell-shocked, as if the sudden intrusion of the dog had knocked him off kilter. He cradled his wounded arm to his chest, and crimson blood bloomed across his white shirt. His face blanched at the sight of it and suddenly, he bolted for the door.

"Stop him!" Ali cried as he shoved her so hard out of his way that she slammed painfully into the doorjamb.

But this time the passerby outside was the conspiracy theorist with the aluminum antenna hat. He peered at her, frowning like *she* was the crazy one, then kept on walking.

"What is wrong with these people?" Ali cried.

She righted herself and looked out the door. Mr. Moon was running along the boardwalk, taking the opposite direction of her bakery's. His figure was shrinking as he pushed people out of his way.

She was about to take off after him when a sudden whimper came from behind her.

"Scruff!" she cried, remembering the dog and his act of heroism.

Filled with anguish she ran back inside the store to tend to him, throwing herself to her knees beside the furry, crumpled heap.

"Oh Scruffy," she cried, tears blurring her vision. "Are you okay? You saved me!"

The straggly pup whimpered as she petted him.

"Please be okay, Scruff," Ali continued. "Please."

Just then, the pup began to unfurl himself from the curled-up position he was in. He drew himself to his feet, wavering momentarily on the spot, then shook himself as if trying to get rid of rain drops.

Relief flooded through Ali. "Oh, Scruff," she gasped. "You're alright."

The pup fixed his intelligent, dark brown eyes on her, let out a small *gruff-gruff*, then bolted for the door.

"Scruff, no!" Ali cried.

The heroic dog had done enough. She didn't want him in harm's way. Mr. Moon might not be armed right now, but he was still a crazed killer with a proven record of hurting people and animals. The last thing she wanted was for her favorite furry friend to get hurt. Two close calls in one day were two too many. She didn't want him to put himself in any more danger than he already had.

She jumped to her feet and ran back to the door.

"Scruff!" she cried out of it. "Come back!"

But it was too late. The dog was weaving his way through the legs of the tourists in hot pursuit of Mr. Moon, who was staggering along the boardwalk.

Just then, Ali realized where she was standing. She was right beside the part of the beach where she'd first found Vincent Cole's lifeless body. In fact, she was pretty much directly above it. The ice cream parlor was positioned just above the shadowy space where the victim had been dumped. Mr. Moon hadn't gone far when he'd disposed of his victim. He'd practically dumped him beneath his own front doorstep!

But there were no cops on the beach anymore, and Ali realized with bitter irony that Detective Elton must have instructed them to clear out after arresting Thiago, incorrectly thinking she'd caught the killer and the case was closed. And not only was there no police presence on the beach anymore, but the two detectives were probably tied up at the station right now, interrogating the wrong culprit. Which meant the only person who knew who the real killer was was Ali herself. And right now, he was getting away.

Without wasting another second, Ali staggered out onto the boardwalk after Scruff, and started to run.

As soon as the sticky soles of her sandals started slapping against the boardwalk, Ali felt a sharp pain radiate from her right hand. She took a quick glance at the purply black bruise blooming across her hand, before quickly putting it out of her mind. There would be time to tend to her battle wounds *after* the killer was caught.

The sun above was setting, making the sky a vivid pink streaked with orange and the ambient light dim, and the boardwalk was busy with tourists heading out to see the sunset. Ali dodged and weaved her way through them, trying to keep one eye on Mr. Moon and the other on Scruff as he galloped to catch up.

Suddenly, she slammed right into someone's back. "Sorry!" she cried.

She was about to dart past them when she realized *who* she'd bumped into. It was her father!

"Dad?" she exclaimed, drawing back. "What are you doing here?"

"I thought you might need help carrying the ice creams back from the parlor," her father said. But in an instant, his gaze began to rapidly dart all over Ali's face and his expression fell. "What's wrong?" he cried, taking her by the shoulders. "What's going on?"

"It's the ice cream seller!" Ali spluttered through her labored breathing. "He killed Vincent Cole!"

Richard blinked with surprise. "The ice cream seller? Mr. Moon?" He frowned with confusion. "But you said they arrested Thiago."

Ali shook her head, desperate to get her father to understand what she was telling him. "I was wrong. It's not Thiago! It's Mr. Moon! And he's getting away!"

Richard Sweet needed no further convincing. For all his foibles and misgivings, all signs of disbelief disappeared from his face, and to Ali's great relief, he snapped into action.

"Which way did he go?" he asked.

Ali pointed along the boardwalk, the throbbing pain radiating from her right hand getting worse as she did. "That way. Scruff's following him."

"Leave it to me," Richard said and went to dart off.

Ali stopped him with a hand on his arm. "I'm coming too."

Richard grimaced, but only briefly. In the short time he'd spent in Willow Bay, he must have learned that his daughter was not one to shy away from danger, nor take instructions.

"Okay," he said relenting. "Let's go."

They took off along the boardwalk side by side, weaving through treasure hunters and tourists in their desperate pursuit. But when they reached the final two stores on the boardwalk—Miriyam's rival bakery *Kookies* and Fat Tony's pizzeria—they screeched to a halt.

"He's gone!" Richard cried.

"Not so fast," Ali said.

She pointed down at the boards beneath their feet at a trail of fresh crimson blobs. Her father frowned, clearly confused.

"Blood," Ali told him. "Scruff bit Mr. Moon earlier. He's leaving a trail. It will lead us right to him."

Richard's face lifted into a smile. "What a clever dog."

"Clever and brave," Ali agreed. "Look, the trail goes that way, onto the beach."

She pointed and she and Richard followed the splotches as they veered to the edge of the boardwalk. At this part of the beach, there was quite a jump to get down to the sand. Two heavy boot prints marked the spot where Mr. Moon must have landed, and more red splatters added to the evidence.

"He went this way," she said, hopping down and landing on the pale golden sand with a soft thud.

A moment later, her father jumped down too, landing beside her heavily. He wasn't as sprightly as he'd once been, and she had to remind herself he was an older man, less robust than the man in her memories.

"Now where?" he asked.

Ali put a finger up to her lip, gesturing to her father to remain quiet. Then she pointed with a trembling finger to the shadowy crawl space under the boardwalk, showing him the trail of blood that indicated where the fugitive had gone. "He's heading back the way he came," she whispered. "Under the boardwalk."

She shuddered, remembering the moment she'd discovered Vincent Cole's body. Mr. Moon clearly had a fondness for the dark shadowy place he'd hidden his victim. Now he was using it as a hiding place. An escape route.

Silently, Richard nodded his understanding. He nudged a cell phone from his pocket and Ali recognized from the sparkly red, gem-encrusted case that it was Piper's. There was no time to ask why she'd lent it to him. He held it up to show her that he was dialing *9-1-1*.

Ali nodded, then mouthed, "I'm going in."

Richard grasped hold of her arm, stopping her. "No!" he whispered. "It's too dangerous."

"Scruff's in there," Ali whispered back. There was no way she was leaving her beloved dog to face this creepy psycho all on his own. Especially after he'd so heroically saved her life. "Wait here for the cops. Someone needs to show them where to go. You can track me on the app."

Seeming to understand, Richard flashed her a reluctant look of defeat, then let go of her arm. Gulping, Ali ducked beneath the boardwalk.

Straight away she was hit with the horrible, dank smell of rotten wood and seaweed. She wrinkled her nose in disgust. The crawl space was a horrible place to be, even without dead bodies and murders to worry about. She shuddered to think of how many creepy crawlies had made this damp, smelly place their home.

145

She walked slowly, taking cautious steps. It was too dark beneath the boardwalk it was impossible to see properly, and with the constant thud off footsteps overhead she couldn't even use her hearing to help. She was without her two most important senses at the most crucial moment of her life—while on the hunt for a killer!

Suddenly, Ali felt something soft against her ankle. Her skin prickled as she thought of a rat. But then she realized, no. Not a rat. *Scruff.* The dog had found her and was silently pressing himself against her ankles as she walked. For reassurance? For guidance? Either way, she was beyond relieved to know he was unharmed.

But a split second after feeling relief, something suddenly moved in front of her, and Ali's terror returned tenfold. Lurching toward her was Mr. Moon!

Scruff barked feverishly as Mr. Moon launched himself forward to grab her. Ali staggered back, losing her footing. She landed with a thud onto her backside. This time when her hands hit the ground she felt the sharp pain and screamed out, knowing instinctively the snapping sound she'd heard before in the parlor had been one of the bones breaking.

Panting in pain and terror, she looked up at the dark figure of Mr. Moon looming over her. He had no weapon — the first knife left at the scene of Vincent's murder and now taken into evidence, the second lying beneath the counter of his ice cream parlor where it had fallen — but that didn't seem to stop him. Instead, he lurched at Ali with his bare hands.

Everything happened in a flash. Scruff pounced on her chest, growling and snapping his jaws at Mr. Moon's hands. Then suddenly someone barreled into Mr. Moon's side, tackling him roughly to the ground.

Gasping with shock, Ali's first thought was her father, that he'd abandoned his *9-1-1* call when he'd heard her scream and had put himself in grave danger. But no. The man wrestling with Mr. Moon was not her father. It was Detective Callihan.

"Sebastian!" Ali cried, relief washing through every fiber of her being. She felt the tenseness whoosh out of her body and a sudden fatigue overcome her.

Detective Callihan wrestled the ice cream seller face down on the ground, pinning his arms behind him while jamming a knee into his back. As the man bucked and writhed like a bucking bronco, Sebastian turned to look at Ali and grinned.

"Miss Sweet," he said. "Fancy running into you again."

Ali felt as if her entire body had turned to noodles. The shock of it all. Of Sebastian being there. Of the killer being caught. Of hers, and Scruffs, and her father's lives no longer being in danger. It all culminated inside of her turning her body to jelly.

But she just managed to keep herself upright long enough to look deeply into Mr. Moon's eyes. "Why did you do it?" she asked him. "Why did you kill Vincent?"

"He ruined my grand opening," he replied through angry clenched teeth. "Then came in bragging about the coin. I killed him in the barber's chair and stole the coin for myself!" He began to laugh in that horrible demonic way again, and Ali realized that Mr. Moon was a real-life Sweeney Todd in the making.

Just then, she heard footsteps coming from behind, and a moment later, the hunched form of Richard appeared in the crawl space. He was leading a group of cops behind him.

A flashlight was shone into Ali's face. She held her hand up to shield her eyes.

"Don't worry, boys, I've got this," Detective Callihan said. He snapped handcuffs around Mr. Moon's wrists. "Mr. Moon, you're under arrest for the murder of Vincent Cole."

CHAPTER TWENTY THREE

Ali sat at the window seat of her bakery, swinging her legs beneath her. Through the window—which was thankfully no longer obscured by a disgusting porta-potty—she could see Piper fussing over Scruff, petting him and feeding him scraps while she called him a hero. Seth and Delaney were also there, listening with rapt attention to Richard as he recounted his version of events for the cops. The flashing lights on the top of the police car illuminated the now dark boardwalk. A few stray detectorists were lurking around with the curious seagulls trying to see if anything exciting was going on.

Inside the car, looking brooding and furious, sat Mr. Moon. Outside of the context of his ice cream parlor his fancy moustache looked rather ridiculous.

"Here," came Detective Callihan's voice from above her. "For your wrist."

Ali tore her gaze from the window and looked up. Sebastian was holding out a pack of frozen berries he'd taken from the bakery's freezer. He'd wrapped it in a cloth like a makeshift ice pack.

"It was the best I could find," he added, apologetically.

"Thanks," Ali said, taking it from him and holding it to her sore, swollen hand. It had ballooned to double its usual size and was an angry red color. Her thumb was purple and blotchy.

"I really think that thumb might be broken," he said, sinking down beside her on the window seat. "Can I take a look?"

Ali's heart fluttered from his proximity and from the anticipation of physical contact. She held her hand out to him and watched with rapt attention as he took it gently in his and started inspecting it. Warmth from his fingers radiated into her hers.

"So you've been in Haven Bay this whole time?" she asked, discovering a timidness in her voice that had not been there before. "Working on Thiago's stolen bullion case?"

He nodded. "Kind of a funny coincidence huh? I get drafted to the next town along to help solve this case that was dragging on, while you and Elton are back here in Willow Bay chasing down the same suspect."

148

"I mean, I wouldn't say there was a 'me and Elton' in this investigation. I was mainly keeping out of her way."

He smirked. "Sure, you were keeping out of *her* way. But she was clearly following what you were doing. How else do you think she ended up at *Thiago's?*"

"I thought so," Ali replied, shaking her head. "I thought maybe she'd been trailing you."

"Nope," he joked. "Pretty sure I came as a total surprise."

Ali peered back out the window and Mr. Moon. "Don't you need to get him down to the station?"

"Meh. He can wait."

She turned back and smiled at him. "I still can't believe you're here. When Detective Elton said you were helping another force, I thought you'd be gone for ages. But you solved the case just like that." She clicked her fingers.

Sebastian shrugged in his understatedly self-assured way. "Whaddya know."

She couldn't help but feel a surge of pride. She'd always known Sebastian Callihan was a great detective, she just hadn't known how great. "You know I was really worried at first. Detective Elton wouldn't tell me where you were. I couldn't stop wondering about drug busts and gangs."

He nudged her, playfully. "You worried for no reason."

"I can see that now."

A silence fell and they both dropped their gazes to their feet. Ali, who had a tendency to slip into coyness, decided instead to stay bold. Maybe she'd done more than break her thumb when she slipped on the ice cream? Maybe she'd hit her head as well and had a concussion that was giving her confidence. Or *maybe* she'd just realized if she could face off against a murderer, she could tell Sebastian how she really felt about him…

"It wasn't just that I was worried," she said to his profile. "I missed you."

He looked up, sharply, as if surprised. "You—missed me?"

"Yes. You've never not been here. Through all the tough times. And the good ones, too." She paused, realizing as she spoke just how much she meant the words, just how true they were. A hundred things seemed to have gone wrong for her since she'd moved to Willow Bay and opened the bakery, and through them all Sebastian Callihan had always been there, like a solid rock. He hadn't flip-flopped like Nate. He hadn't got scared and backed away like Seth. He'd just patiently waited until she was ready to notice him. "I didn't realize how much I needed you here, until you weren't anymore."

Sebastian's eyebrows slowly rose up his forehead. He obviously hadn't been expecting her to be quite so forthcoming. "Oh." A blush began to color his cheeks pink. Ali wondered why it had taken her so long to realize just how adorable he was.

She nudged him with her shoulder. "So, Sebastian Callihan...what are you going to do about this?"

"About what?"

"About my confession."

He smiled and scratched his neck. "What do you want me to do about it?"

Ali shrugged a shoulder. "Well, for starters I think you need to apologize for disappearing on me like that and leaving me to solve the whole crime without you." She was teasing him. Or flirting. Or both. Whatever it was, it felt extremely natural, and Sebastian did not seem to mind one bit.

"But you did it so well without me!" he joked. "You even managed to not get arrested by Detective Elton."

"I mean, there was one hairy moment..."

He laughed. "Alright, okay. I'm sorry. If I'd had the choice, you know I would have chosen to be here."

"Good," Ali replied with mocking haughtiness. "So how are you going to make it up to me? You've been saying for a while now that you're going to take me on a date." She was flirting, which was something extremely alien to her. But it seemed right and natural to do with Sebastian. "Dinner? Wine? Flowers? Something along those lines..."

"How about this?" he said, leaning forward and planting the softest, most tender kiss on her lips.

Ali's heart soared. "That's...a good start..." she murmured, before a sudden pain shot through her thumb. "OW!"

"Sorry!" Sebastian said, wincing with empathy as he jumped back from her and looked down at the blotchy thumb that he'd accidentally squished. "I — it's — yeah that's definitely broken, Ali. We should get you to the hospital so someone professional can take a look at it."

He stood up, offering her his arm. She took it and he helped her to her feet.

Just then, the sound of blaring sirens came from outside. They both looked over in time to see the bakery door fly open and Detective Elton storm inside.

"Callihan!" she bellowed. "Step away from the witness!"

Ali couldn't help herself. She started to laugh. "You know there's no law against detective's dating, don't you? You've got to stop interfering in Seb's personal life."

"I have no problem with what he does in his personal life, but this behavior is completely unethical while he's on duty!"

Sebastian gestured to his civilian clothes. "I'm not on duty."

She frowned. "You were at the station with me."

"Working on a different case for a different department. Who let me leave since we'd caught the right guy. Speaking of which..." He pointed out the window at the cop car and the angry Mr. Moon glowering in the back seat. "That's your bad guy."

Detective Elton stood there, arms folded, a pout on her lips. She was clearly unhappy. But even she had to concede that on this occasion, she was in the wrong.

"Just don't let any of this mushy stuff happen while you're on the clock."

"Deal," Sebastian replied.

Detective Elton marched back out the way she'd come to speak to the cops and take a look at the actual culprit in her investigation, and Sebastian turned back to Ali, holding his arm out to her. "Shall we?"

Ali rested her good hand on his and allowed him to guide her out of the bakery.

The evening air had cooled considerably with the fading sun. As she emerged onto the boardwalk, everyone who'd been waiting around turned to look at her.

"Ali," Delaney said, reaching her first, before even Scruff. "How is your thumb?"

"Broken," Ali told her.

Her friend gave her a sympathetic look. "You poor thing. If there's anything I can do to help let me know. A lift to the hospital? A drink? Anything?"

"Oh Delaney," Ali said. "What did I ever do to deserve such a great friend like you."

But rather than smile, Delaney's eyes fell to her feet, as if with shame. "I'm not a good friend," she muttered.

Ali frowned. What was she talking about? "Delaney. Come on. You're the best. Everyone knows it."

Delaney shook her head and to Ali's surprise her shoulders started to shake with soft sobs. Ali's heart lurched for her. "What's going on?" she said, softly, rubbing Delaney's bare arm with her good hand.

Just then, Seth stepped into her eyeline. "It's me," he said. "Us." He put an arm around Delaney's shoulder. "We're dating. We didn't know how to tell you."

Ali paused, her mind going back to the moment in the bakery when her father had mistaken them for a couple, and the awkward look they'd shared. Then she thought back even further to when she'd bumped into Seth on his way into *Little Bits of This and That.* He'd seemed strange to her. And now she knew why.

She looked back and forth between them, from Seth's dark eyes to the side of Delaney's tear-stained face. "That's... that's... AMAZING!" she cried.

They both looked at her, stunned.

"What?" Seth asked.

"Is that sarcasm?" Delaney asked. She knew how Ali and Teddy often slipped into sarcasm, much of which went over her head.

"No!" Ali cried. "I'm actually happy for you! Thrilled!" She threw her arms around both of their necks, pulling them into a strange, awkward, three-way hug. "You know I think you're both awesome. Why wouldn't I want two people I adore to find love with each other!"

She let go of them. They were both still looking stunned, but at least the fear had left their eyes.

"Did Seb give you something for that broken thumb?" Seth asked. "Something strong."

"Nope," Ali said. "I'm genuinely happy for you guys." She looked over at her Dad waiting beside the cop car. "Life's too short to hold grudges."

Finally, her two friends seemed to accept what she was saying, and Delaney snuggled into Seth's side as they walked away.

Her dad approached. "Ali....you didn't tell me you have a boyfriend?"

Ali blushed. She had no idea what she and Sebastian were, and now wasn't the time to define the relationship. "Dad, this is Seb," she said, evading his question. "Seb, this is my dad."

While most men might have freaked out about meeting the father of their crush, Seb took it all in his stride. He reached out a hand to shake Richard's. "Nice to meet you, Mr. Sweet. I'm afraid I have to take your daughter to the hospital. She has a broken thumb."

"Oh no!" Richard said, looking worried.

Ali felt a surge of something inside of her. "Actually, Seb, do you mind if my dad takes me. I'll let you take me next time I break something."

"Of course," Sebastian replied, laughing. He kissed her, softly. "I'll call you."

He headed off, leaving Ali with her father.

"That's the look of love if ever I've seen it," Richard said, as he watched him go.

Ali smiled to herself.

"So, Dad," she said, looping her arm through his, this time. "Let's go to the hospital. You and me. And maybe once my thumb's been seen to, we can think about a good time to have that talk. I was thinking over dinner. Wine. Pizza. How does that sound?"

Richard smiled at her gratefully and patted her hand. "That sounds like a very good idea."

*

The doctor flipped through the pages on his clipboard. "Your blood pressure is a little low. So are your potassium levels. Have you been eating properly?"

Sitting on the hospital gurney, her broken thumb now in a cast that seemed unnecessarily big, Ali cast her mind back over the whirlwind last few days. Skipped dinners. Sabrina's unsatisfying croissant. "Wow, no I really haven't," she confessed.

"And I'm not happy with your hydration levels. What's your fluid intake been like?"

She gave him a sheepish look. "Does coffee count?"

He sighed. "That depends on whether you're using it instead of sleeping. How's your sleep been?"

Ali glanced over at her dad who was snoring in a big chair beside the bed. Like her, he'd been up before dawn to bake. She looked back at the doctor. "Non-existent."

He flipped the clipboard shut. "I'd like to keep you in overnight to be careful. Put you on a drip. You're suffering from exhaustion."

"Oh," Ali said, surprised. She'd not even realized how much she was running herself ragged. "I don't know if I can. I have a dog." Poor Scruffy. She hoped he wasn't sitting outside her apartment waiting for her. It would be a long, lonely night.

"Maybe send your father to look after the dog," the doctor said, nodding to her dozing dad. "It's important you stay here. I guess we'll be using the left hand for the IV."

Ali looked at the cast on her right. "Yeah, I think that's for the best."

Just then, the curtain to her cubicle was drawn back and Teddy came rushing in.

"Ali-cat!" he cried, running to her and throwing his arms around her. "Piper messaged me to say you were being taken to the hospital!"

Ali held up her cast. "It's just a broken thumb. Ow!" She looked over to see the doctor had jabbed her IV in while she wasn't looking.

"Then what's that for?" Teddy asked, sternly.

"I'm dehydrated. That's all. I promise you, Teddy. I'm really fine."

Teddy put a hand to his chest. "Oh that Piper and her melodrama."

Ali laughed. That was rich coming from Teddy!

Just then, a solemn expression came over Teddy's face. Ali realized he'd spotted Richard dozing in the chair in the corner.

"Teddy-bear," Ali said, resting a hand on his arm. "I know you're mad, but for me, please don't start an argument."

Teddy patted her hand and nodded his agreement. Just then, his phone began to ring.

"Uh, it's Hannah," he said. "I messaged her after Piper messaged me and she probably thinks you've been in some terrible accident as well."

"Answer it," Ali told him. "We need to tell her about dad anyway."

As the cellphone in Teddy's hand kept ringing, Richard stirred in the chair and opened his eyes. "Oh," he said, looking at Teddy. "Hello, son."

"Hi," Teddy said. Then he turned around and answered the call. "Hannah, don't panic, Ali's fine. She's broken her thumb and is super thirsty or something and—what? What do you mean you're at the hospital? *This* hospital?"

Ali's eyes widened. She couldn't believe it. Hannah lived in New York City. What was she doing all the way in California? Surely she had come here just to see her!

"You were at a stopover in LAX for a business trip," Teddy continued. "I see."

Ali looked over to her father, suddenly worried about how this unexpected turn of events might affect him. He'd come to the hospital to take care of his youngest daughter and now had his son who hated him on the phone to the daughter who was indifferent toward him. Having all three Sweet siblings in one place would be enough to send the sanest person running for the hills. But far from looking concerned or perturbed, her dad looked... happy?

She looked back at Teddy who was still speaking into the phone. "Yes, fourth floor, that's right. But Hannah, listen, before you get here you need to know that—"

It was too late. At that moment, the powder blue curtain surrounding Ali's little cubicle was tugged open and Hannah came careening inside in a tight gray business suit, cell phone attached to her ear, high-heeled stilettos clacking on the hospital's tiled floor. She had been dying her naturally strawberry blond hair jet black for as long as Ali could remember, but now she'd had it cut into long-bob, and hung in a straight, severe line that accentuated the shape of her chin.

Ali couldn't remember the last time she'd actually seen Hannah in the flesh; and she was struck by the same sense of unfamiliarity she'd felt on seeing her dad for the first time. Hannah didn't even attend Christmas at their mom's anymore, since she always traveled to China with her husband and sons to visit his elderly relatives. Had she been there for Thanksgiving? Ali couldn't even remember, now. Her appearances were so rare, so few and far between, she really gave Richard a run for his money...

"Ali," Hannah said, lowering the phone. She was frowning, but there was nothing unusual about that. Hannah always frowned. "Are you okay? What happened?"

"I'm fine," Ali said, holding up her cast. "I broke my thumb. That's all."

Hannah pointed at the IV drip. "What's that?"

"I'm also a bit dehydrated," Ali told her. "But honestly, Hannah. It's fine. You really didn't have to come all this way."

"I have a twelve hour stopover in LAX," she said, bluntly. "I thought I may as well." She halted suddenly, her gaze finding Richard sitting in the seat in the corner for the first time. "Oh. Dad's here."

It was the most Hannah thing to say that Ali couldn't help but smile. And though it was the simplest statement in the world, it held so much within it.

"Hello Hannah," Richard said.

"Surprise," Teddy said sheepishly.

"Surprise?" Hannah repeated. "Not really." She perched on the edge of the bed and kicked off her heels. "Mom told me all about Ali's search." She tucked her legs up beneath her and peered at their dad like he was some kind of peculiarity in a museum. "I guess you found him. How are you, Dad?"

Richard looked at each of his three children in turn. "I couldn't be happier."

Ali felt his words strike right into her heart. Never had she ever thought this would happen again, the four of them together like this. Behaving civilly.

"I should break stuff more often," she murmured. "If it gets all of us in the same place at the same time."

Teddy sank onto the bed beside Hannah. "You always were the glue in the family," he said, tenderly.

Ali was touched. She'd never really thought of herself that way. But seeing all the disparate parts of her family come together in one place for her made her feel it deep inside.

She looked at her dad. "You know with all three of us together, now might be the best time to talk about what happened. About why you left."

She'd been expecting some sort of kick back from her siblings, but instead they both remained silent, neither in agreement or disagreement. Ali suspected that like her, they were just tired of wondering.

"Alright," Richard said. He leaned forward resting his hands on his knees and took a deep breath. "Well, I don't know how much your mother explained about the divorce, but it was more or less amicable. I lost my job and, well, I was happy. I realized I'd been stuck in this dead-end, stressful job that I hated. I wasn't in a hurry to find another one and after a while your mom got fed up."

Ali had had no idea about her dad losing her job. She'd been young and it had clearly gone right over her head.

"After the divorce, things were okay for the most part. I lived off my severance and some odd jobs and rented a little apartment nearby."

"I remember it," Hannah said. "There was a palm tree in the yard."

"That's right." He smiled. "But the money ran out eventually and... well... I suppose I was ashamed. I couldn't buy you presents or contribute to your hobbies or after school clubs. Drama, swimming, piano, your mom paid for all of that. I felt useless. And the less I got involved the more I realized how useless I really was. You were all getting by just fine without me. It was selfish of me, but it started to hurt too much and I... I took the path of least resistance." He gave them all a sad smile. "I guess it's just in my nature."

Silence fell.

"It wasn't because I came out?" Teddy asked.

Richard looked up at him, genuine pain in his eyes. "Teddy, no! It was nothing to do with that at all. I'm proud of you, of the person you are. You didn't really think...?" A look of devastation flashed across his eyes as it finally dawned on him why his son had been so frosty all this time, why he'd never had the desire to rebuild their bridges.

"I always thought it was my fault," Hannah said. "I knew you and mom were arguing over money. I figured it was because I demanded to go to such an expensive college."

Richard looked at his eldest daughter, shaking his head. "No, Hannah. No. We always had enough savings for your education. That was never the problem."

"I thought it was me," Ali said. "After graduation. We had that huge fight and I said I never wanted to see you again."

Richard shook his head. "No, Ali. It wasn't that. It was nothing any of you did. It was me. All on me. I'm so sorry you thought even for a second that it was you."

The three siblings glanced at one another. It wasn't them. It had never been them.

A great weight seemed to lift from her shoulders.

"So I have news," she suddenly blurted, her voice a welcome release from the profound moment."

"Oh?" Teddy asked.

Hannah looked at her expectantly. "What?"

She looked at Richard and grinned. "Dad's helping me open a restaurant."

EPILOGUE

Ali leaned across the table and jabbed her fork into a piece of steaming Parisian gnocchi, before putting it into her mouth. Creamy flavors flooded her mouth. "Mmm. Yes. This one. This is definitely going on the menu." She scrawled on the paper beside her, her handwriting still messy from the weeks she'd spent with her hand in a cast.

Sebastian pointed his fork at the gnocchi suspiciously. "I'm not sure. They don't taste right to me. Are you sure that's gnocchi? It tastes more like Chinese dumpling."

"It's *Parisian* gnocchi," Ali told him. "It's made differently to the Italian type."

"I see, I see. But I still don't understand why you won't serve calzone. Everyone loves calzone!"

"Because," Ali said, "I want to keep the theme French. It would be an insult to my old mentor Milo Baptiste if I served something *Italian* at my restaurant!"

"And it would be an insult to your boyfriend if you didn't," he teased.

Ali laughed and gave him a kiss. "Sorry, buttercup," she teased right back. "But I want *La Patisserie Sweet* to be authentic. You don't get many chances to launch a new business in life, and I want this one to be perfect to make up for the disaster of the bakery. But I'll make you calzones at home for dinner."

"Promise?" he asked.

"Promise."

A NEW SERIES!

NOW AVAILABLE

A VILLA IN SICILY: OLIVE OIL AND MURDER
(A Cats and Dogs Cozy Mystery—Book 1)

"Very entertaining. Highly recommended for the permanent library of any reader who appreciates a well-written mystery with twists and an intelligent plot. You will not be disappointed. Excellent way to spend a cold weekend!"
--Books and Movie Reviews (regarding *Murder in the Manor*)

A VILLA IN SICILY: OLIVE OIL AND MURDER is the debut novel in a charming new cozy mystery series by bestselling author Fiona Grace, author of *Murder in the Manor*, a #1 Bestseller with over 100 five-star reviews (and a free download)!

Audrey Smart, 34, is a brilliant vet—yet fed up by her demanding clients who think they know more than her and who don't care about their animals. Burnt-out with the endless hours, she wonders if the time has come for a new direction. And when her 15th year high school reunion (and her hopes for re-sparking on old flame) end in disaster, Audrey knows the time has come to make a change.

When Audrey sees an ad for a $1 home in Sicily, it captivates her. The only catch is that the house requires renovation, something she knows little about. She wonders if it could be real—and if she may really be crazy enough to go for it.

Can Audrey create a life and career—and the home of her dreams—in a beautiful Sicilian village? And perhaps even find love while she's there?

Or will an unexpected death—one that only she can solve—put an end to all of her plans?

Are some dreams too good to be true?

A laugh-out-loud cozy packed with mystery, intrigue, renovation, animals, food, wine—and of course, love—A VILLA IN SICILY will capture your heart and keep you glued to the very last page.

Books #2 and #3 in the series—FIGS AND A CADAVER and VINO AND DEATH—are now also available!

Fiona Grace

Debut author Fiona Grace is author of the LACEY DOYLE COZY MYSTERY series, comprising nine books; of the TUSCAN VINEYARD COZY MYSTERY series, comprising seven books; of the DUBIOUS WITCH COZY MYSTERY series, comprising three; of the BEACHFRONT BAKERY COZY MYSTERY series, comprising six books; and of the CATS AND DOGS COZY MYSTERY series, comprising six books.

Fiona would love to hear from you, so please visit www.fionagraceauthor.com to receive free ebooks, hear the latest news, and stay in touch.

BOOKS BY FIONA GRACE

LACEY DOYLE COZY MYSTERY
MURDER IN THE MANOR (Book#1)
DEATH AND A DOG (Book #2)
CRIME IN THE CAFE (Book #3)
VEXED ON A VISIT (Book #4)
KILLED WITH A KISS (Book #5)
PERISHED BY A PAINTING (Book #6)
SILENCED BY A SPELL (Book #7)
FRAMED BY A FORGERY (Book #8)
CATASTROPHE IN A CLOISTER (Book #9)

TUSCAN VINEYARD COZY MYSTERY
AGED FOR MURDER (Book #1)
AGED FOR DEATH (Book #2)
AGED FOR MAYHEM (Book #3)
AGED FOR SEDUCTION (Book #4)
AGED FOR VENGEANCE (Book #5)
AGED FOR ACRIMONY (Book #6)
AGED FOR MALICE (Book #7)

DUBIOUS WITCH COZY MYSTERY
SKEPTIC IN SALEM: AN EPISODE OF MURDER (Book #1)
SKEPTIC IN SALEM: AN EPISODE OF CRIME (Book #2)
SKEPTIC IN SALEM: AN EPISODE OF DEATH (Book #3)

BEACHFRONT BAKERY COZY MYSTERY
BEACHFRONT BAKERY: A KILLER CUPCAKE (Book #1)
BEACHFRONT BAKERY: A MURDEROUS MACARON (Book #2)
BEACHFRONT BAKERY: A PERILOUS CAKE POP (Book #3)
BEACHFRONT BAKERY: A DEADLY DANISH (Book #4)
BEACHFRONT BAKERY: A TREACHEROUS TART (Book #5)
BEACHFRONT BAKERY: A CALAMITOUS COOKIE (Book #6)

CATS AND DOGS COZY MYSTERY
A VILLA IN SICILY: OLIVE OIL AND MURDER (Book #1)

Made in the USA
Las Vegas, NV
14 March 2023

69094072R00095